On the Breakaway

 Formatted with Vellum

On the Breakaway

Contents

Fairy Godfather

Sugar and Spice and Everything Nice

Behind the Stick

Home Ice Advantage

HARPER ASHLEY & WREN HAWTHORNE, NICOLE BANKS,
MOLLY DOYLE, KAT FALLONS, LAUREN GREENE,
EDEN KNOX, DJ KRIMMER, K. ELLE MORRISON,
L. RENEE RICHARD, K.M. RINGER,
JENNIFER J. WILLIAMS, ZOEY INDIANA

LOVE SICK

a valentine's anthology

Introduction

This is the one that started it all.

Late in 2023, K.M. Ringer put out a call in the Hype Girls Discord channel for authors interested in participating in a Valentine's Day charity anthology. Up until this point, I had watched my author friends organize and create beautiful anthologies, and I hadn't been brave enough to try — until now. The mission, should we choose to accept it, is simple: Write a short story, around 25,000 words, centered around love in which ever vision we see fit. Promotion would ramp up to release on February 13, 2024, published on Amazon, and would go out of print 6 months later. Royalties would go to Trevor Project.

Within our author group, discussion and emphasis circled around "Hearts, not parts," something Molly Doyle had quipped at one point. It embodied everything we wanted to express in our stories. We had gummy bear shifters, throuples, polycules, body positivity, and through it all? It was all about being in love, and sharing love. And with all that in mind, Love Sick was born.

Love is love. Full sentence.

Within Love Sick, I had "On the Power Play," an MFM, body positive love story. I knew I wanted to stay close to the Ice Wolves/Sin Bin Series world, it just felt natural to keep within the team dynamic. The bones of the story were solid: She's been dumped right before Valentine's Day, and her ex's teammate shows her that the holiday doesn't have to suck. Cool, simple enough. The one hiccup I ran into was it didn't feel like a "one and done" story — they had way more than 20k to tell me — and also, it felt like there was a puzzle piece missing. As an author, we always say we're at the mercy of the characters and what they say. As soon as I committed to "Love Sick," I had three characters in my ear. Three? This was a new experience, having more voices than I had originally planned on, but as soon as I started fleshing out who went where, it made perfect sense.

I already had Robicheaux and Kozlov kicking around in my head because they had small cameos in "Tripping for Number 68," which had just released the previous summer, and already had future books and plans on the horizon. While they weren't giving me "we're together-together" messages, I also couldn't figure out how to give them each their own book in the series. It just didn't feel right, like only wearing one shoe. I played with this one as a way to work out if this is what they really wanted. Go figure, what they wanted was to start a poly relationship with Bridgette! Putting them together was as easy as breathing.

Having Kozlov's "black cat" vibe balancing Robicheaux's "golden retriever" gave me this amazing balance within the relationship. And in the middle of this? Bridgette. She was a whole new addition to the Ice Wolves family, but I loved it. She loved her body and had amazing confidence, but the breakup with Chad may have bruised it just a little bit.

Before I had my first draft finished, I knew I needed to

make a full novel for their story, and immediately penciled in "On the Power Play"— the full novel— as book 4 in The Sin Bin Series.

Don't hate me; that one is going to be a ride, with all of the feelings involved.

Love,

Eden

Chapter One

Bridgette

Well, that was fast. Not surprising in the least, outside of the break-neck speed, that he found a puck bunny to replace me. *Stupid Valentine's Day, stupid bunnies, stupid jocks with no taste in anything.* Cursing at myself, I stared at Chad Parish, our fourth line center and my now ex-fiancee, from the opposite end of the tunnel. His large frame wrapped around her smaller one, and she looked like she was trying to climb him like a tree. I questioned my life choices: why did I ever think that it was a good idea to date him, and where was the appeal?

Spinning on my boot heel, I headed for the exit. I had to get out of here before he saw me. I didn't need to see his cocky grin on his ridiculously handsome face, and I most definitely didn't want to see that skinny little puck bunny hanging off of him. *Hell, I didn't even give him back my engagement ring yet.* The garishly large rock flashed from my left hand. My plan was to hand it off to him now, but clearly he's too busy.

I should have known better. Dad told me that dating

players was a horrible idea. They're temporary in our world, when an injury can cut a career short or when time with a team is measured by the year. With him at the helm, I'm the princess in the Ice Wolves' kingdom, and he rules everything. Not that it ever stopped Chad from being a disrespectful asshat. For the longest time, I wondered if he only dated me because I'm Bridgette Marie Andrews, eldest daughter of Team Owner Roger Andrews, and what it might do for his career and not because he actually liked me.

"Bridgerton! What are you doing down here?" Robicheaux's voice carries from the hall across from me.

I squeak, trying to duck back around the corner before Asshat and his bunny could look my way. Looking down the hallway at them, I see he's pulled his face away from her but he hasn't looked my way. *Thank goodness, I really don't want to deal with this right now.*

Jean-Luc Robicheaux came onto the team in a trade package with Kozlov, but had been friendly to me from day one. His upbeat personality made team events more fun, and often, when Chad stood me up or left me alone, Roby was there to pick me up. I couldn't deny that I regretted saying yes to Chad because I've been completely unavailable for someone as caring as Roby. Would I have been this miserable if I avoided the Chads and found him instead? As much as I mourned my engagement, I can't deny that I feel lighter, freer now.

He lightly jogs toward me, still blind to the scene around the corner that was unfolding behind me. I stick a finger to my lips, telling him to be quiet. In true golden retriever mode, he skids to a halt, his head tilting to the left in confusion and making his black curls flop in his face. Pointing down the opposite hallway, I prayed he would understand what I was wordlessly saying. He approached the corner from his side, and peeked around like I had. The kaleidoscope of emotions that overtook his features was dizzying – confusion, shock, and anger being the strongest. His jaw and his fists clenched, and I panicked when I saw him start to walk out into the hall.

I slash my hand across my throat, trying to keep him from moving. A dark eyebrow lifts as though saying *oh, you think you can tell me what to do?*

I pull my phone out of my pocket and drop him a short text:

> Don't do anything. I just need to get out of here without him seeing me and pretend I didn't see this.

Pulling his phone out of his back pocket, he glanced at my message and nodded before typing and then staring expectantly at me. I looked down at my incoming messages and read,

> Roby: You trust me, right? I'll take care of it. Come over here.

I froze. I couldn't cross the hallway, he'll see me. I watched Roby step forward, and lean against the wall, his pose relaxed, hands in his pocket. There was no doubt he would be directly in line of sight of my ex. He glanced down the hall again, before lifting one large hand my way, and crooking a finger. *Come here,* he motioned.

Taking a deep breath, I tried to shake off the nerves I was feeling.. I could do this. I walked out from my hiding spot, slowly approaching him. He pointed to a spot right in front of him. *Come stand here,* he motioned. I stepped forward to where he indicated, looking back up at him. *God, he's so damned tall.*

"Trust me?" he murmured. I nodded, looking at him. "Good. Just follow my lead, eh?"

Before I could respond, he wrapped a hand around the back of my neck, pulling me the one last step between us, and pressed his lips to mine. Fireworks exploded. I gasped into our kiss as my hands lifted to grasp the lapels of his jacket. The hand that had been so casually tucked into his pocket wrapped around my back, sliding up my spine. I felt my toe pop – Jesus, was Roby giving me that "toe pop kind of kiss" from Princess Diaries? My head spun with all of the sensations.

"*Merde*," he whispers against my lips, grasping my hair in his right hand and pulling my head back, dropping a hot kiss on my neck.

"Bridgette? Is that you? What-" Chad calls out. "What the fuck? Roby?"

"Don't say anything." His words are muffled against my neck.

"Okay," I whisper as he rocks my head back to his shoulder so I still can't see if Chad is coming toward us.

"What's up, Turtle? Didn't see you down there." I snort against Roby's neck, knowing that Chad was sensitive about his somewhat respectable 5'10" height, but Roby had a solid 6 inches on him. And that nickname, he detested it. He may have earned it by shoving one of the league's biggest defenders, before dropping to the ice in a little ball before they could properly fight it out. Almost a year later, and "Turtle" stuck.

"What the hell are you doing with my girl?"

"*Your girl?* I heard you broke off your engagement, so that makes her definitely *not* your girl. And besides, who's that over there with you?" I feel him move a hand away, and could just visualize him flicking that hand dismissively at them. "She looks more like your girl than Bridgette from this angle. Face it, you lost your shot and I picked up your rebound. I think I'll hang onto her for a minute, if she doesn't mind."

My head is spinning, I can't wrap my head around what's going on. Robicheaux is clearly stating that he wanted something. And why is Chad just now getting upset about it? He didn't care when he agreed to call off our engagement!

"Damnit, Roby, what about The Code! No touching someone's sister or girlfriend!"

That's it, I've heard enough from him. Stepping out of Robicheaux's space, I turn to face my ex.

"I stopped being your girlfriend when you said I was too fat to take out in public, asshole! Here, take your damn ring and your puck bunny, and go." I slide the ring off my hand, throwing it in his general direction, not caring where it went, hearing his curse as he hunted it down. "Roby, let's go. I don't want to stay here anymore."

"Certainly, *ma cher*, anything you want." With a gentle hand, he guided me back toward the locker room and away from Chad. "Let's go in here first. Take a minute to breathe." Opening the door, I walk in, skirting around the logo in the carpet and collapse bonelessly on a bench.

"Happy Valentine's Day, huh?" I say, looking up at Roby who was still near the door.

Shrugging, he replies, "I don't know, it might have some high points to it." I scoff, looking back down at my now bare left hand. "The night is still early, anything could happen."

"I failed at being a girlfriend, my engagement is

irreparably broken. I'm not sure where there's a positive in that."

"Well, you're no longer weighed down by the Turtle, how about that? You are now freed up of 275 pounds of deadweight douche."

I frown at his usage of the word. "Awesome. He always wanted me to lose weight, just didn't think it was going to be all of him."

Robicheaux froze. "You don't mean any of that...do you?"

"He pointed it out a lot, honestly. It's seriously part of the reason why he broke off the engagement. I was 'too much' for his tastes."

"Were you really too much, *ma cher*, or was he not man enough? I think the perspective is off. You have so many better options to work with than him."

I smile, looking up at him and his wide open face. "You're always so sweet, and say all the nicest things. Thank you, I appreciate it, even if it's just lip service to keep me from crying in the team locker room."

"Who said it's just lip service? We're just getting started, beautiful girl," he says with a wink, pulling his phone back out of his pocket. A few swipes of his phone, and he pressed it to his head. "Koz, you ready to go? I pissed off the Turtle. Yeah, yeah, it was worth it though. We're taking Bridgerton with us. No, she doesn't...yeah, I know. I'm sure. Okay, I'll meet you at the car."

My heart sinks a bit as I realize that wherever we were going, Kozlov would be coming with us. I know they carpooled to the arena, and last I knew they were splitting a condo together. The fact that most likely, they came tonight together, wasn't a surprise. After all of Roby's declarations a moment ago, it's a bit of a downer.

"It was sweet of you to save me from Chad earlier, but you don't have to–"

"I don't have to do what? Do you think I did that back there just for show? He didn't know what he was doing with you, and you're way too good for him. Hell, I'm not sure if I'm even good enough for you, but I sure as hell want to try."

"Oh, Roby..."

"Koz is my winger, my best friend, he knows..." he trailed off, a restless hand sliding through his floppy curls. "Look, I've been waiting for you to break free from that *fils de pute* so I could finally ask you out. I know your breakup is still fresh and I pushed my luck earlier, but I just had to try. I won't apologize for it."

I'm in shock, honestly. I had no idea how he felt. "You never said anything–"

"What was I supposed to say? That I want you to dump my teammate, even if he's a cheating dickhole and he deserves it? All so I can have you to myself? You wouldn't have wanted to hear it like that from me, love."

"Well, yeah, that would have been nice to know," I mutter, crossing my arms under my chest, uncomfortable with the words being spoken out loud. Assuming it happened was one thing; hearing it confirmed is another. "So, now what? Where do we go from here?"

"First, Kozzy is picking us up. Then, we're going out to dinner because we're both starving athletes, and I know you haven't eaten yet today so we're going to feed you. Then we'll see where the night goes." He shrugged while stuffing his hands in his pockets again, shuffling a foot on the carpet. "No pressure, no plans tonight. You can say how long or short the night lasts. Just what feels right, eh?"

Chapter Two

Robicheaux

My heart is racing, not like it does after running skate drills with Coach, but close. I hold her gaze, refusing to be the one to break eye contact first. I'll be damned if I lose my chance. I've sat back, watched her waste time with this dick who didn't even appreciate her, and stepped up when he dropped the ball. I was the one who chatted with her and danced the night away at the charity gala when Chad couldn't bother to show up for her. I was the one at Moxley's engagement party who talked to her and tried to make her happy again when she saw him standing too close to a puck bunny, and dried her tears when she later heard the same bunny describe in explicit detail just what he looked like naked.

How anyone could treat Bridgette that way was beyond my thought process. She was the sweetest, most caring person around the organization. Even before she began working in the upstairs offices officially, she made sure every incoming player felt welcome. Her heart is so pure, and Chad tried so hard to dull her shine. Goodness like that can't be tarnished. Not to mention she looks like a goddess. I wanted to run my fingers through her auburn hair to see if it was as soft as I imagined. I dreamed of making her smile until her dimples popped and her cheeks flushed. Her curves were dangerous. I've lost count of the number of times I've seen her by the bench and nearly wiped out during practice like I'm back in Mites again. Bridge is my kryptonite.

Kozzy knows it too, I'm sure he's going to have something to say tonight to push my buttons in front of her. He's the ballsy one, going for what he wants. That's why he's a forward, always trying to get the upper hand. He's a great balance to me on wing, we read each other on ice like a synchronized machine. Off ice, he's my other half; the cold to my hot, the logic to my impulsive nature. That's why we're best friends and roommates, on the road and off. He is the closest person in my life that isn't blood related, and I trust him with my life.

She ponders my statement, the caution visible all over her face. While there's no reason for her not to trust me specifically, her trust in general has been shaken. I understand, and if she told me right now that all she wanted was to go home by herself, I would tuck her into an Uber and watch her go. Seeing her still standing there, though, makes me wonder if she doesn't want that scenario at all.

"You said Kozlov is picking us up? Why?"

"We carpooled to the arena, and we're still sharing the condo." She nods, her brow furrowing again.

"So, what does he think is happening tonight?"

"He thinks we, the three of us, are going to dinner. We were going that way anyway, like normal, but we would love to take you with us. He's fond of you as well, you know."

"He's a good guy," she murmurs with a smile. "Fine, you talked me into it. Where are we going?"

Internally, I celebrate, fist pump and all. "It's Kozzy's turn to pick which probably means steak is involved. You're okay with that, right?"

Her shy nod tells me everything. I know Chad had her limited to grilled chicken and salad at all of the team dinners we've attended, and I've watched her eyeball Kozzy's plate more than once when she thinks no one is looking.

Holding out my hand to her, I wait for her to place her smaller hand in mine and escort her out to the parking garage. She's actually coming with us, and I'm so damn excited about that. We have to treat her gently, I know, because she's still fragile, but she deserves to be pampered and appreciated, especially on Valentine's Day.

True to his word, Kozlov is standing beside his truck, waiting for us. I recognize the moment he sees our linked fingers, his gaze laser focused on them before his eyebrow quirks up. I can just about hear the thought that accompanies that action: "That's an interesting change of events. We're going to talk about this later." He opens the passenger door as we approach, and holds out his own hand to help her up into the truck. I hand her off to him, allowing my hand to graze across her lower back as she contemplates how to get up into his behemoth of a vehicle in her heels.

"Come here, *koshechka*. Hands on my shoulders." She does as she's told, placing her hands slowly on his broad shoulders.

"Kozzy, I'm too heav–oh!" she exclaims as he lifts her from the waist to put her up on the seat.

"I know what you were about to say, and I won't have you speaking of yourself like that." His brisk tone brooked no argument. "Please buckle up, and I'll get the door for you. Get in the back, Roby, I'm starving."

It feels so natural for the three of us to get into the vehicle and leave together, and we ease into friendly conversation. Pulling in front of Kozzy's favorite restaurant, I see her stiffen slightly as he pulls in front of the valet stand.

"Oh, I didn't think you'd, um, here...crap." She looks out at the entry of the restaurant, where people are milling around in the brightly lit space. The sidewalk in front of her door is right under a bright flood light.

"What's wrong, Bridge?" I ask, watching her twist her fingers nervously. "I told Kozzy he needs a stepladder for this freaking thing. We'll get one next time."

"It's not– okay, it's partly that. But this is where Chad had...," she trails off. "Chad had told me before we broke up that he had reservations here for Valentine's Day, and I don't really want to run into him."

"Fuck Turtle," Kozzy growls. "I'll get him removed if he bothers us. I'm not giving up our dinner because he's a pest. Besides, the owner loves us," he motions between us, "and can't wait until that dick gets traded. So let's go enjoy our night. Now stay still, I'm coming around to get you out."

Without another word, he slides out of the driver's seat, and shuts the door. I stay put, reaching up to rest a hand on her shoulder. "It's going to be fine, B, okay?"

Her smile is tentative, and my heart cracks realizing just how badly he's damaged her. Our girl– it's surprising how it feels really great to say that– needs careful handling for now, but I just know she's going to rise from his ashes.

Kozzy opens her door, blocking the opening with his size. Dude is a human door when he wants to be. Tentatively, she turns and tries to step onto the running board with her heel. He frowns a bit before resting his hands on her booted ankles, setting the balls of her feet on the board. He looks up at her shocked sound, before grasping her hands, placing them on his shoulders, and then resting his own hands on her hips.

"*Odin, dva, tri,*" he prompts before lifting her from the seat and setting her down on the ground, a soft growl escaping him as I see she slides down the front of his chest, her coat riding up between them.

"I'm sorry, I didn't mean to," she mutters, looking down, her cheeks going pink in her embarrassment. She goes to step out of his reach but he follows her, their movement allowing me room to open the back door and get out.

"*Nyet,*" he argues, shaking his head. "You are perfect."

"But you, you made a sound and I'm not exactly light–"

"Bridge, babe, I've spotted him in the gym. He's really fine. Besides, that's not his 'I'm lifting heavy weights' sound. That's–"

"Shut up, Roby."

Her eyes dart between us as Koz wraps up with the valet, and we start toward the door. She's silent as we check our coats, greet the hostess, and walk to our table. We flank her, protecting her from the people milling around. I hope we can block her from seeing Turtle, where I spot him getting settled at a table as well. Her steps falter a bit, and I realize she's made eye contact with him. Damnit, that's not at all what we needed. My hand rests on her lower back, providing some support for her as we go, and I stare down the prick before I realize my hand isn't the only one on Bridge's back. *Atta boy, Kozzy,* I think to myself as we make it to his preferred table.

As we get settled and the hostess walks away with our drink orders. She again looks between us, sitting on either side of her. Kozzy, in his usual way, smooths the linen napkin precisely across his lap before shifting his water glass to the opposite side of his plate.

"So," she starts, playing with the condensation on her water glass. "What was it then?"

"What was what?" Koz asks.

"If that wasn't because I was heavy, why the sound?"

I snort on the water I had started to sip before she talked. Oh, shit. She totally called him out.

Chapter Three

Kozlov

My head tilts and I look at her, wondering what exactly she's talking about. Sound? Did I say something rude?

"What sound?"

"You made a sound when you helped me out of the truck. I know that I'm heavy and I'm sorry I made you strain yourself."

She has to be shitting me. I glance at Roby, gritting my teeth at his wide-eyed goofy grin behind his napkin.

"Zamolchi! Der'mo," I hiss at him, slashing a hand across my throat to tell him to cut it off. Her gaze narrowed. He just chuckled back, sitting back in his chair with a slight lean toward her. Damned hyperactive golden retriever, he can't play the long game and he's the one who says I'm aggressive and goes for what I want? Bull.

"Want to hear a secret?" He stage-whispers, and I roll my eyes at his antics. Zero chill off ice, this one.

"Roby. Dial it back." The last thing she needs is to be jumped on as soon as she's single. She turns her eyes to me while still leaning into Roby's side.

"What kind of secret?" She whispers back, never breaking her eye contact with me.

"Our big Russian here has also been waiting for Turtle to fuck up."

"Well, he definitely did that," she murmurs, picking up her wine glass. Her eyes keep drifting over to where he's sitting, his obnoxious laughter breaking the enjoyable din of the restaurant, and I want to do nothing more than kick his ass out of here for making her uncomfortable.

"Bridgette. Look at me." Her gaze locks on mine. "We're not wasting any more time on him tonight. He's not worth your thoughts, your words, anything. Tonight is about you and what you want. Do you understand me?" She nods. "Good girl." I watch her eyes drift shut a little. "Oh, you like that, do you?"

A pretty blush stains her cheeks and she ducks her head, breaking our eye contact. "I'm sorry, it's just… it's nice to hear on occasion."

Without thinking, I tuck a finger under her chin, tilting her head to look back at me. "Let's play a game. You can tell us to stop whenever you want, but I want you to be honest with me the whole time. *Da?*" Roby has been leaning closer, elbows resting on the table, the entire time I've been talking to her. His wide eyes are on mine, waiting for word. It wouldn't be our first time playing a game like this, but this time the stakes are way higher. This isn't just a bunny after an away game.

I feel her chin lift and drop over my finger. "Good, now come here." With the slightest pressure from my finger, she leans toward me just enough that I can touch my lips to her cheek. Her breath catches at the touch, and I grin as I ease closer to her ear. "We've been waiting a long time for you, *koshechka.*"

"You– you have?" Her voice is breathy as I lean in, breathing the warm vanilla scent of her perfume. She makes a soft noise, and I can feel more than I can see Roby moving closer on his side as well. Perfection, I think as I drop a kiss against her neck.

"Told you I wasn't the only one," he says and I can sense him on the other side of her neck. "You good, B?"

"Great, actually. Except for regretting not dumping him sooner," she chokes out in a laugh. "God, I can't concentrate when you do that." We both chuckle on either side of her, and Roby mutters a "sorry" before pulling back slightly, and tucking her hand into his. "Oh, don't be sorry, just...wow. I had no idea how you both felt about me."

"You should've heard that one going on," I breathe in her ear as I run my finger along the impression where her engagement ring used to sit on her ring finger. "Pretty sure he actually pouted about it."

"That's adorable," she sighs. "And you?"

"Don't let him fool you," Roby responds, and I look over to see him lift her other hand, pressing a soft kiss to her knuckles. "I heard him calling in favors to get his ass caught, because maybe then you would break up with him so we could," he pauses, considering his words, "talk."

"Come on. You miss 100% of the shots you don't take, The Great One said so," I shoot back. "Besides, a good offense outsmarts the defense every time, so I had to outsmart, outplay, outrun the opposition. I'd say it still worked better than pouting."

"Boys," she laughs, before cutting it off with a small cough. "Um, guys, what are we doing? Anyone can see us here. I mean, Chad–"

Pulling back to look at her just as Roby places a finger over her mouth, I notice her gaze across the room. Fuckface was eyeballing us while talking to his puck bunny, a smirk on his face. He thought this was funny? He had no idea.

"We're not going to worry about him, *koshechka*. He can sit over there and laugh because you know what?" I pause, watching her attention pull back to me from him. Leaning in again, I whisper, "We know the truth, don't we? We know that he's going to take her back to his place where she'll experience the most mediocre sex of her life. Meanwhile, Roby and I are prepared to take you home and pleasure you until you pass out, wake you up, and do it all over again. We want to worship you like the goddess you are. We won't stop. You know how competitive we are, it's going to be a race. Who can do it for you first, faster, more. We'll make up for the suffering you've endured with him." I run my finger along the hem of her skirt.

"I...I don't understand. You've wanted me the whole time. Why?"

"Why not?" Roby asked. "What is not to like? You're sweet, you're gorgeous, and the things I – or we – would do to you are too numerous to count. We would have pursued you earlier if it wasn't for Turtle."

"Jesus Christ, Bridgette, whoring around out here where anyone can see? Pitiful," Chad's voice carries across the din of the other guests. "And not just with one, but two other players? What will everyone think? Sleeping your way through the roster? Two at a time, because there's enough of you to go around? If this is what you were planning, I'm glad I left you."

I watch her pale, looking ill, before her cheeks flame red in anger. *That's our girl,* I think, as she stands up and looks him up and down.

"You're the pitiful excuse, Chad. Who's your date? Did you get her name this time? And maybe it's not that I'm too much for one guy to handle, maybe it's just that you weren't man enough to take care of me. Get out of my sight, you disgust me." She stares him down, watching him turn on his heel without another word. Behind her, I motion to the maitre'd to remove him and his party. God, I love having fans some days.

Bridgette sits back down at the table, placing her napkin primly in her lap and taking a deep breath. "My apologies, if you need me to leave, that's fine. I deserve that."

"What you deserve, *cher*, is a proper Valentine's Day without that douche interfering. Come on, let's enjoy our dinner. Okay?" Roby's soft tone and comforting touch on her hand help her to relax, and we ease into conversation as our meal begins to arrive.

Watching her enjoy her steak without the brow-beating and snide comments from that idiot pleases me. I order in dessert while she's distracted, and grin as her eyes widen when we're presented with an array of tiny desserts.

"There's so much," she whispers in awe. "There's no way, it's so rich, I couldn't–"

"B, relax, babe. You can have as much or as little as you want."

"Honestly, we usually split them every time because that one," I nod at Roby, "can't make a decision for anything. So splitting everything into 3 bites is not that big of a differ-ence. May I?"

She nods her head jerkily at me and watches with wide eyes as I split all of the little desserts and set a sliver of triple chocolate cake with ganache frosting on my fork. I hold it out for her. Waiting for her to make the first move. She eyes the desert, tempting her, and looks at me, as though waiting for me to take it back. I move it closer.

"Take it, *minette*, you'll thank me later," Roby chimes in. "That one is my favorite, it's so good."

Decision made, she reaches out with one tentative hand, holding my wrist steady, before taking the proffered bite. Her eyes drift close and a soft sound leaves her lips before she swallows. "Oh my God, that's amazing," she says, sitting back in her chair.

"I think I might have a new favorite, Roby."

"I told you that one was better than sex. And you're planning to top that one somehow?" Roby takes up his fork, reaching for my favorite, the strawberry cheesecake, and offering her a bite. "This one is his favorite. He might be offended if you don't like his choice as well as mine."

"I don't get offended," I grumble, looking at the rest of the plate. "There's something to be said about mine. It's straight to the point, and you know exactly what you get."

"You're not wrong, Kozzy, and both are amazing," she responds diplomatically. "Honestly, I really like both."

"But you have a favorite. What would you get every time if you could?" Roby's question seems innocent enough, but I've watched him enough to see him question his stance.

"Honestly? The chocolate cheesecake, with strawberry, and a drizzle of chocolate sauce. It's like both of yours combined." She points to the one that sat between our respective choices. The answer was simple, honest. Gathering the chosen one in the middle, I hold it out to her. With less delay this time, she takes the bite from me, moaning happily. "That's the best one. You need to try it."

"B," Roby whispers. "You're killing me with those sounds."

"Oh. I'm sorry, I didn't realize–"

"Don't you dare stop." I cut her off. "You're enjoying

yourself, da? That is the important part. Your enjoyment, your happiness. How else can we make you happy."

"I– I don't know if– I mean," she stumbles over her words.

"No judgment, no pressure. Remember, B. You can tell us."

"I'm not sure where to begin."

"We can help you with that," I answer. "You want to hear our thoughts first?" She nods, and I grin at Roby. "I, to start, have been watching you for months, and knowing I could make you happier even on my worst day."

"That's quite the start, Koz." Her voice is raspy and soft. "And you, Roby?"

He leans in close to her. "I've wanted to know what a man like me has to do to get you to look at him. How can I be the one you depend on for anything."

I watch her lean into his side as he talks, and double back down. "We've watched and waited for our turn to care for you, and wondered if you would give us the honor of cherishing you." A soft whimper escapes her at my quiet words. "We've wanted to know if you're wearing thigh highs under this skirt for months." I feel her nod. "Oh, so Roby's right? Maybe he should be the one to find out."

"Please let me, B, baby," he whispers, asking for permission.

"Can we go home first? Please?" Her plea is soft, but I can see the warring emotions on her face. The desire is there, but so is the trepidation that someone will say something again.

"We should take this home. Let's go, Roby."

Chapter Four

Bridgette

My head spins as I think about where my night had started, and where it is heading now. I thought I would be dropping off my engagement ring and then spending the rest of the evening at home, questioning where I had gone wrong and why the hell I wasn't enough for Chad. Now, though, I had a whole different list of questions in my head. How had I missed that Robicheaux and Kozlov both wanted me, and was I actually entertaining the idea of what a night with both men would be like? I had heard talk that they did "everything" together. It wasn't a secret that they've shared living quarters since their college days, but there were whispers that they also shared women, as well.

Walking out the door with Roby to my left and Kozy to my right, I smirk as I feel Chad and his new girl's eyes on me, their attention specifically on the large hands at my back. Good, eat your heart out. Standing together while waiting on Kozzy's truck, my heart races with the possibilities of what is going to happen next. His truck pulls up, and

I move to the front door before Roby tugs me back against him.

"Come back here with me," he says, opening the door for me. I slide in with a smile, waiting for him to get in as Kozzy moves around front to get in the driver's seat. Without realizing, I tentatively lean closer to Roby when Kozy pulls the vehicle into traffic. "I've been wanting to do this since the arena," he mutters as he pulls me closer, kissing me soundly as his hand tangles in my hair.

My eyes drift shut, but not before I make eye contact with Kozzy in the rear view mirror. His gaze is hungry, but I relax into Roby's embrace anyway. His hands are everywhere, one at the back of my neck, the other sliding restlessly along my side, toying with the edge of my skirt without crossing the boundary between us. I grab that wrist before it can repeat the motion again, and rest his fingers below the hemline.

"You're sure? Say please." His hand holds perfectly still, waiting for permission to move forward.

"Yes, please," I moan against his lips. He's driving me crazy with his delicate handling.

"Handle her like you mean it, Roby, our *boginja* wants it," Kozzy growls from the front seat. So bossy, but something about his tone makes me shiver. He pulls up to a red light, turning to look at us in the back. "Lean forward, he's had all of your kisses so far."

I do as I'm told, bracing myself against the front headrests and lifting slightly from the middle seat to press my lips to his, only for him to kiss me as if his life depended on it. His tongue licked the seam of my lips, before easing in to dance with mine. Roby slides his hands up my thighs, making me gasp in surprise.

"Green light, Koz," Roby called out behind me, making

Koz break the kiss so he could go back to driving. "Fuck, that was hot to watch."

"You should see you two back there. Tell me about those stockings, what is our girl teasing us with tonight."

I bite my swollen bottom lip, looking at Roby for support. He nods his head toward Kozzy, as though saying, "tell him." His fingers dance along the silky material, teasing higher. "It's– it's a whole matching set. I didn't expect anyone to see them, but they made me feel pretty. I like to wear pretty things."

A growl fills the cabin from the front, and Roby looks at me intently as he eases a finger along the collar of my shirt before pulling it away slightly. "Oh my God, Koz."

"Color?"

"She's wearing our team color, man." Roby grins at me, triumphant, as he takes a look at my light blue lace set. Sure, it's also the team color, but who doesn't feel pretty in pastels?

He curses from the driver's seat, and I giggle, feeling my cheeks heat. Never, ever did Chad treat me like this, like something to be treasured.

"How far are you from the condo?" My voice doesn't sound like mine as I ask.

"Almost there, babe. Come over here." He slips a hand under my knee, lifting me to straddle his thick thighs. I squeak at the sudden change in direction, but gasp as I feel him twitch under me. "See what you do to me? You have us both so wound tight it's crazy." I shift a little, trying to find my balance while not resting completely on him. "Nuh-uh, baby girl, sit down."

I could feel myself panic. "But—"

"I said," he said with a growl, "sit. The fuck. Down." With firm hands on my hips he pulls me down against his lap, grinding us together. "Don't make me beg for it. Now kiss me."

I followed his instruction, leaning forward and kissing him. Kozlov slows the vehicle down, coming to a stop. Before I know it, he's turning off the engine and popping out of the driver's seat before the engine falls silent. Roby held me firm against his lap, the contact setting off tingles. The door popped open beside us and brisk air made me shiver.

"Let's get her inside and comfortable before we freeze to death." Kozlov said, sliding a hand up my back. "Besides, keep this up and the neighbors are going to complain." With a quick move he lifted me off Roby's lap, pulling me out so fast I had to wrap my legs around him to hang on like a koala. "That's better," he growled, turning to take long strides to the front door.

"Those boots are killing me. They're staying on tonight, I mean it." Robicheaux walked past us on the walkway, unlocking the door and holding it open for us. "Fucking ridiculous how hot you are in them, Bridge."

"Stockings stay on then, too, you know." My quip is cut off with a squeak as Koz starts to drop me with a curse but he recovers, resetting me around his waist before pressing my back against the wall, grinding his hips into mine.

"Tease, you're going to pay for that one." He cut my gasp off with a quick kiss, then we resumed the trek up the stairs.

"You can put me down, you know," I say in a giggle, laughing harder as he growls. "So dominant, I swear."

"You have no idea, B. I don't think he'd even switch, but I would pay good money to watch you work him over." Roby's statement carries to me from a few steps behind, and

I can't help but wonder if this is a regular lifestyle dynamic for them.

"You just want to have an excuse to top me."

"Maybe, but I'm sure you'd enjoy it."

"Are you two," I gasp when Koz places a kiss on my neck. "Always like this?"

"Nah," Roby responded. "Let's just say you bring something special out in us."

Before I can dig into this one any deeper, Koz lays me down on a bed carefully, my boots dangling off the edge. Without exchanging a word, they stretched out on either side of me, Koz pressing a sweet kiss to my shoulder as Roby shifts my head toward him for another deep, drugging kiss like he gave me in the truck. I pressed my thighs together restlessly as hands moved across me, working in tandem to unbutton my shirt. Feeling the cool night air on my over-heated skin, I pulled my head away from Roby enough to look down, seeing Koz slowly moving the two halves of my shirt apart, breathing in deep before lowering himself to one breast.

"I never want to see you in another color. You belong in our colors." He presses a kiss to the top of one cup, at the edge of the light blue lace. "You'll only wear our jerseys." He leans across to kiss the other. "Or nothing at all." He shifts down, placing a series of open mouth kisses across my ribs, and then down the center of my stomach. I move to protest, trying to pull his head away because even though these two are being really sweet and I'm enjoying everything, all I can hear in my head is Chad's voice saying how gross I am, how he didn't want to have sex with the lights on, how—

"*Koshechka*, come back to me," Koz says softly, his head

hovering over mine. When did he get there? "Where did your head go?"

"I—" I pause as I feel Roby sit up to look down at me as well. Embarrassment courses through me, and I screw my eyes shut. If I can't see their pity it isn't there, right? Without thought I wrap my arms around my waist, trying to feel smaller still. "I'm sorry. I know what it looks like and it's sweet of you to try and make it not a big deal—"

"Bridgette, love, look at us." With a shaky breath I pull my hands away, looking down into their two eager faces. "You're beautiful, and we adore you. All of you. I don't care what he thought, he was wrong. You know that, right? His opinion doesn't matter. I adore you. Kozzy does too even though he may not say it with words. Let us show you tonight, please."

Looking between them, I feel safer and more cared for than I have in months, if I was honest with myself. I nod, a whispered "okay" on my lips.

"Trust us, *koshechka,*." Koz slid a hand down my stomach, playing with the waistband of my skirt. "We'll take care of you and this little cocktease of a skirt. This is all I'm going to think about when you're prancing around the arena in your short skirts and boots, and then what I'm going to do to you later. Won't be able to focus on the coaches because I'll be distracted by this." I feel my skirt slide down my legs, and look as their eyes widen at the same time. "Roby?"

"Yeah?"

"Take care of our girl."

Robicheaux gives me one last long kiss, before trailing kisses down my torso, dropping to his knees on the floor, and then kissing the sides of my knees, just above where the leather of my boots stopped. "I love you in these boots. Every time you wear them I'm a mess."

"Roby, I've worn them like once or twice a week since fall!" I feel his hummed agreement against my thigh, as his fingers play with the edge of my stockings.

"I am," he pauses to slide kisses along the zipper, "fully aware," he kisses along the other zipper, "of how often you wore them."

Koz, who has climbed off the bed during this to walk behind me, leans over my face. "Trust me, he's not kidding. I had to hear it every time you wore them and he came home horny and frustrated." His lips closed on mine, swallowing the surprised gasp. "He may seem like a sweet golden retriever puppy most of the time, but you've had him wound up so tight recently."

"I should make it up to him." I gasp as broad fingers toy with the thin straps of my panties, and I look down to see Roby grinning at me as he slowly slides them down my thighs.

"Oh, he's going to collect on that right now," Koz chuckles as Roby holds my thighs wide, winks, and then lowers himself to me. I gasp as he swipes at me with his tongue, devouring me in a way that I'd never dreamed of before. My back arched and Koz's fingers made quick work of my bra strap, exposing my breasts to his view. "Beautiful." His murmur is reverent, and he throws his own shirt off before stretching out to pay attention to my exposed nipples.

"Shit, Koz," I moaned, reaching up to grip his hair, holding him closer. My hands flex restlessly in both of their hair, directing their heads.

"Tell us what you like, kitten," Koz demands between swipes.

"More," I gasp. Roby growls as he doubles down on his efforts.

Koz sits up on his knees and begins working his belt loose, just inside my reach. "You want more, beautiful? Say it."

"Please, may I?" I slide my hand down his stomach, feeling the springy hairs on his treasure trail, as I touch the waistband of his jeans and trail my fingers along the zipper. His eyelids drift close a little as he looks down at my hand, sliding along the outline of his erection. He made quick work of unfastening his jeans, before placing my hand around his swollen shaft. I shiver, he's definitely larger than Chad, thick and long. I shouldn't have been surprised that both Roby and Koz are large, seeing how much taller than me they are, but feeling the heavy weight against my palm, I momentarily wonder if it's too much.

Roby was shifting around below the edge of the bed, removing his clothing quickly before resuming his torture on my overheated body. The tattoos on his massive arms and shoulders rippled as he moved, throwing my legs over his shoulders with one hand. My breath escaped me on a sigh as I took in his focused look, and where was his other hand?

"What are you – are you–"

He pulls back slightly so I can follow the line of his arm down to where he has a grip on himself, leisurely sliding up and down, giving himself a bit of a squeeze just at the head. "Just keeping it warm for you, babe. Koz, man, you need to feel our girl. So good."

"You can enjoy her first, I have another idea. Let me see your pretty mouth, koshechka." I lick my lips in excitement, shifting my head closer. He runs his thumb across my bottom lip. "I love this color on you. Will it look even better wrapped around me?"

Chapter Five

Robicheaux

She's here. She's fucking here and I'm wearing her gorgeous thighs as earmuffs and I'm about to blow. And maybe that's okay right now because no one can see it while I'm down here, but what kind of rookie mistake would it be to cum on the side of your leg when you finally have the most beautiful woman in the world at your mercy?

I hope she doesn't notice how I'm shaking, I know I am. I just want to take care of her and keep her forever, I want her to stay. I want us to be the one she comes home to and I know how ridiculous it sounds because she just seriously got dumped like a week ago by that dick, but I've wanted nothing more than this for months. I know Koz can see it, too. We've talked about it before. We may not have exactly the same feelings about her. Where he admires and respects her, I would gladly put a ring on it and fill her with my baby right fucking now if she wanted.

My eyes roll as she grabs another handful of my hair; I didn't think I was into that but when it comes to her, I don't think there's much left on the list. *Focus, dude,* I tell myself, pulling my eyes to look up at her at the same moment Koz is running his finger over her bottom lip. I groan, watching them together is just so good. To distract myself, I focus on Bridge, seeing what sounds I can draw out of her while she gets up close and personal with him. I can't help but grin when I crook my finger just right, causing a domino effect where she clenches on my hand, locks her heels behind my head, moans around Koz's dick and makes him hiss at the same time. So I do it again. God, I could do this all damn night if she'd let me.

"Will you quit edging her and get to fucking already?" Koz growls, staring me down from his knees. I take one last long, leisurely lick, dipping my fingers in one last time before rising to my feet. I know we need the condoms from the drawer, but before I get that far – "Show me what she tastes like, J."

I slide my knee onto the bed, holding out my still wet fingers to him, a move we've done before. He surprises me, though, and grabs my wrist with one hand, my head with the other, and sucking her arousal off of my tongue. I can hear Bridge moaning below us, and I jump as she grasps my dick tighter than expected. He slowly lets go of my head, turning to look down as Bridge shifts to alternate between wrapping her lips around each of us, one at a time.

"That's probably one of the hottest things I've seen," I murmur, looking down at her.

"I was thinking the same thing," she retorts, shifting so she was kneeling between us. She kissed us both softly. "What happened to the competition?"

"Next time. This time is all about you. Roby, go on. Take care of her."

Reaching into the nightstand drawer and pulling out the box of condoms, I rip one off before tossing the box in

Koz's general direction. No point in putting them back anytime soon.

"Pop up on your knees, baby, please." She obeys quickly, and I just pause taking in the gorgeous view before me.

"Such good manners," Koz praises me, and a shiver goes down my spine. Damn him and knowing my buttons. Bridgette looks back at me over her shoulder, giving her hips a little wiggle at me. She's going to be the death of me, I'm sure.

Putting on the condom takes more concentration for me than it ever has in the past. Breathing deeply, I focus hard. This needs to be right, and I need to not finish the moment I fuck her for the first time. I look up at Kozzy, hoping he gets me. I feel so oversensitized right now that I'm going to lose my shit as soon as we start, and I absolutely can *not* do that to her. This has to be as close to perfect as possible. She deserves it.

"Roby, please," she begs, leaning back toward me. I slide my hands along her soft curves.

"Shh, *minette*, we'll get there." I rest on my knees between hers, the leather of her boots sliding along my calves. Sitting back on my knees, I pull her back onto my thighs, reaching around to cup her breasts. "Open up for us, show Kozzy how well you can take me." I slide my knees wider, spreading her own as she lays back on my chest.

"That's it, milaya devushka." I hear his approach, feeling the mattress dip slightly by my right knee and his hand sliding up the inside of her thigh, his fingertips just touching my own as they travel north. "You're dripping for us," he praises, and I can feel him sliding his fingers between us, his knuckles a welcome friction along my shaft before he wraps his hands around me. "Lift her a bit, Roby, let her sit on your cock properly. I want to watch her make a mess out of you."

Her gasp is music to my ears, and whether it's because he's teasing her with my head or the absolute filth he's saying, I'm not sure. As I lower her onto me, inch by inch, I can feel him there. It's never felt like this before, and I'm scared that it will never feel this good again. Sliding my hands up from her hips, I tease her nipples, watching Kozzy's face as he focuses on the motion. He leans in and kisses her, his chest brushing my knuckles, his body rolling against ours. She grinds on me, moaning into his mouth, causing him to grind on us, making me buck up into her. Then the cycle repeats, the tension building in my spine in a way that I've never experienced. I'm going to black out on them, I can tell.

"Fuck, I'm going to come, you feel too good, B!"

"Not yet," Koz growls, and I can feel him working her clit faster. "She comes first, always."

Bridgette lets loose a cry and I feel her clamp down around me. My vision blurs around the edges as I wrap my arms around her waist, pulling her down hard and deep as I lose myself in her as well.

"Merde," I murmur in her hair, smoothing my hands over every inch of her I can, before looking over at Kozzy. "Your turn."

Chapter Six

Bridgette

There is a buzzing in my head and I feel tingles in my extremities as I try to catch my breath, feeling securely held by Robicheaux's strong arms. I feel floaty, and I could live here forever. I can hear them talking over my head, feeling Roby's voice vibrating through my back where it rests against his chest. I open my heavy eyelids and look over at Kozzy, opening the condom wrapper.

"Again?" My question is barely a breath as I turn my head toward Roby, and he softly kisses my overheated cheek.

"Again," Kozzy confirms, squeezing me tight before guiding me to lay against the pillows. "Maybe more than once, I'm down 2-nil and that just can't stand."

"You're keeping score?"

Two masculine chuckles fill the room, and I look between them, Roby moving off the bed to take care of his condom and giving Kozzy a fist bump as he crawls over top of me.

"Not keeping score, really, koshechka, just making sure

you are very," he pauses to kiss my inner thigh, "very," he kisses the opposite thigh, "satisfied." He slides his tongue along my sensitive center, making my back arch. "I'll be gentle, koshechka, but you're still coming for me again."

I squeak a bit as he lines himself up, easing in slowly before drawing back out at the same pace, letting me get accustomed to his larger size. Roby comes back to the bed and lies down beside me, placing a soft kiss on my shoulder. The slow, gentle treatment tugged on my heart, and I could feel the tears stinging my eyes, so I slammed them shut, hopefully before anyone could see. *Pull your shit together, Bridge!*

"Hey, why the tears?" Roby's soft voice made me break more. Kozzy froze, and I opened my eyes to see both men staring at me intently. "Is it too much? Babe, say the word and we can stop, we don't want to hurt you."

"It's not – You're not hurting me, it's just, so sweet and soft, and you're treating me like I'm this delicate thing that will break, and–" my voice cracks.

"Use your words, koshechka. Tell me explicitly what you want and it's yours."

"Don't treat me like I'm fragile. I'm not a doll."

"You don't want soft and gentle? No 'lovemaking' for our little temptress." I'm afraid of the words getting stuck, so I just shake my head. "Not good enough. Say it out loud."

"Please, Koz," I say.

"You're getting both, you know. It's not one way or the other." He slowly resumes his shallow thrusts. "You'll get the hard with the soft, the lovemaking and the fucking, the praise and the degradation. You're getting it all, and then we're going to do it all over again. We aren't just going to fuck you and leave you."

Roby leans in close. "We're going to spoil and pamper

you. You want him hard and fast? He'll give it to you. I have no doubt. But let us cherish you at the same time, oui?"

Koz grabs one of my ankles, propping it on his broad shoulder. "Now, are we in agreement?" I nod, and he accepts the answer, rolling his hips again, picking up in tempo. My eyes roll back, and I feel myself clench around him. Gasping, I try to slide a hand up his hard chest. "You and these cocktease boots, God I love it," he growls, sliding a thick hand up and down the smooth leather. "So damn beautiful, look at you, taking me so well. Roby, touch our girl, get her off."

"On it, Koz." He slides his middle finger between his lips, before trailing it down my torso, circling my clit in time with Koz's thrusts. "Your tits are killer, squeeze them together for us, that's our girl, so good." Roby's praise in one ear while Kozzy's filth rained down in the other was a decadent blend, sending chills up my spine. "That's a good girl, give it to him, wanna watch him really lose his grip on that tight control? Watch this."

With quick movements, he shoved a pillow under my hips, intensifying each thrust, making Koz groan and throw his head back. I moan as the angle changes his depth, ratcheting me closer to my own orgrasm. Without missing a beat, he drops his hand back between us, flicking quickly.

"Koz, Roby, I'm–" I cut myself off with a gasp as Koz slammed deeper, harder, and Robicheaux, evil genius he is, dropped the heel of his palm against my soft lower belly.

Fireworks. I may have left my body. Koz was keeping up his punishing rhythm and I couldn't stop myself from tumbling over that cliff again. This never happened with Chad. Ever. What was I missing?

Cursing in Russian, Koz shouted out his own orgasm, and his spasms triggered my own aftershocks.

"Good girl," Koz praised, leaning forward and dropping a heated kiss on my lips. "And you," he said, grabbing a handful of Roby's curls, "know too many secrets. You'll pay for that one."

"I look forward to it." Roby looks down the length of my body, goosebumps forming over my chilling flesh. "We should get you into the shower and to bed. Tomorrow is game day, I know you'll be busy."

Koz eases off the bed, walking to the small dorm fridge he keeps stocked with water bottles and retrieves three, coming back to the bed to hand us each one, flipping his fingers at us to tell us to drink up, before laying his bottle on the nightstand. He settles on the edge of the bed, bringing my boots across his thighs, working the zippers down my calves. With delicate touches, he slides off one boot and stocking, before repeating the process on the other.

I lean back on my elbows, a soft smile across my lips as I look at him, running his large hands over my bare ankles.

"I'm going to go start the water," Roby says, getting up and taking his bottle with him, leaving me snuggled against Kozzy. There is something about the way they both move to take care of me in their own way, making me feel cherished.

"I'll be right back," I whisper to Koz, kissing him softly on the lips before getting up and walking across the room, well aware that his eyes are on me. Walking into the bathroom as steam starts to rise from the shower, I hug Roby from behind tightly, feeling his broad chest expand on a sigh.

"I can't thank you enough for saving my Valentine's Day."

"Saving your Valentine's Day? I'm pretty sure you made ours. It's a fair trade, I think, cher."

Chapter Seven

Kozlov

"Come here, koshechka," I sigh and pull her into my side, enjoying how her curves feel against me, still warm from the shower. "Roby will spoon you when he comes back."

Her happy hum vibrates my chest under her cheek, and she wiggles closer, throwing her thigh over my own. "Good. I like to be the little spoon."

The bed dips a bit as Roby joins us. He curls his large frame behind her, and I feel one large hand slide between us as he wraps her in his own embrace. Almost at the same time, we all sigh contentedly as we settle in.

"I set the alarm so we aren't late for praccy." Roby's tone is muffled and slurred with sleep.

"You gave us enough time to feed her breakfast, da?"

"Yeah, and to get her home to change beforehand." I can hear him sigh before he grumbles, "why can't we be like this every night. I could sleep like this forever."

I agree with him, I already feel more relaxed than I have in ages, as though the missing pieces in our world are finally clicking together. Maybe we could make this a serious thing, build a whole relationship as a team. We certainly don't want to rush her, but he's right. I could see us here, months and years from now. It's nice to consider.

"Patience, J. You can't shoot from center ice. Watch and wait."

"I know. I just want to keep her forever."

"If I say you can keep me, will you go to sleep too?" she mumbles as she wriggles between us.

"Yes, Princess, he will go to sleep too. Shut your hole, J."

There's a moment of peaceful stillness, where we all sink into the comfort that is holding and being held. Roby is right, I would love to keep her here, just like this, the three of us together. We'll need to talk about it later, of course, but for the moment, we're going to just enjoy ourselves. There is time to figure out the logistics later.

"Kozzy, next time I want to say what happens, you pushy bâtard," he murmurs, just at the edge of sleep.

"Get a hat trick tonight and maybe I'll let you run the show next time."

"Promise?"

"Promise. Now go to sleep before I tell Bridgette to spank your insolent ass."

"Oui, monsieur."

I wake up the next morning in a tangle of limbs, Bridgette's curls in my face, my dick nestled between her cheeks as she curls against Roby's side. I breathe in, smelling Roby's fancy-ass curly shampoo and conditioner in her hair, and smile. Maybe Roby is rubbing off on me, because I think I could wake up like this every day. My quiet moment is broken as Roby's phone blares from the dresser, making the three of us groan at the same time.

"I don't want to get up, I'm warm," Bridgette complains,

burrowing deeper under the covers instead. Our kitten is most definitely not a morning person.

"If you get up and get dressed, I'll have coffee ready for you downstairs, da?"

"Fine," she grumbles, throwing the blanket back over her head so all I can see is a tuft of hair spread across the pillows.

"Roby, can you get our girl something to wear home?" A grunt from the other side of the bed is the only answer I get.

Life with these two will be entertaining, at the very least.

Epilogue

Bridgette

Coming back to work after the ending of my engagement, I had been nervous about how it would feel. Coming in today after spending the night with Robicheaux and Kozlov, however, was not as awkward as I originally thought. As planned, the three of us acknowledged each other as we always had during the day, cordial professionals just passing in the hallways and chatting at team events. I was still very, very aware of their eyes on me because as we discussed at their place, knee high boots and dresses, preferably in team colors, would be their weakness. Who was I to defy orders, I thought to myself as I looked down at my light blue sweater dress and black boots with silver buttons, knowing it drove them crazy earlier during the press conference.

Sitting in the owner's box with my dad, however, was another story. Could he tell I did something with other players? I know he was aware about the issue with Chad, and the end of my engagement. No hard feelings there, he tolerated him for being a decent player but he didn't approve of him as my other half. He offered to trade Chad just so I wouldn't need to see him on a regular basis. While I would love to not see his face anymore, weaponizing our positions in the team like that seemed a bit extreme. So no, Chad is finishing his contract, and there's already been talk with his agent that he's been looking at possible trade options when he enters free agency at the end of the season.

I sip my wine as I look down on the ice, my boys– God, my heart flutters when I say that– are circling their zone, laser focused, and Robicheaux has already scored twice before we made it to the third period. His energy level is off the charts and he's operating like a one-man ESPN highlight reel.

"Damn, that Robicheaux is certainly on fire today. I wonder what got under his skin." Dad's voice boomed across the suite, making me jump, droplets of wine falling on my hand and the toe of my boot.

It's me, I think as I carefully mop up the wine off my hand, biting my lip to keep in the giggle that threatens to escape me.

"Kozlov is playing his A game, too," Bruce Fuller, Dad's accountant, chimed in after a spectacular check into the boards by my big forward. "There's no getting past him tonight."

Kozzy passes the puck to Roby one more time as the last minutes wind down, and I grin as the lamp lights up one more time, and then hats rain down on the ice for his hat trick. I look down as Kozzy raps on Roby's helmet in congratulations after the rest of the team has given him glove bumps and helmet taps. As a matched pair, they both look up at me, and I salute them with my wine glass.

Looks like we'll have our work cut out for us next weekend.

the
cozy
chronicles
COZY AND BOOKISH AUTHORS
2024
A COZY AND BOOKISH ANTHOLOGY

Introduction

"Snow Day" was my entry into the Cozy Chronicles, a charity anthology to coincide with signing at Cozy and Bookish in Miamisburg, Ohio in November 2024. Proceeds from the anthology were donated to a local cancer charity after going out of print.

I brought Mox and Ronni back for this one, because while it was fun to bring Roby, Koz and Bridge out for anthologies, I felt like they had more to tell. A little interlude where they fall back into their forced proximity trope without being stuck at the arena together felt like something they would do. Elliot plotting a romantic getaway where they end up snowed in at a cabin in the middle of nowhere felt very much like an Elliot Moxley™ branded issue. His heart is always in the right place, the execution though? Leaves a bit to be desired.

Elliot's plan for just a weekend at the cabin turning into a whole week stuck together, especially when Ronni doesn't adapt to spur-of-the-moment change well, and still has work to do, felt natural for a moment with them. Poor Mox...he tried.

And just like with Roby, Koz, and Bridgette for both "On the Power Play" and "Sugar and Spice and Everything Nice," there they were. Elliot and Ronni were very loud about all of it, and what they expected to happen. The building conflict where Elliot would need to confess that he didn't believe the weather forecast, which would lead to Ronni confessing that she saw the weather, and okay with the risks, it felt like a landmark moment in their relationship. Clear through Tripping, Elliot was "trying" but it would backfire for some reason, and Ronni would — understandably — become frustrated because of it disrupting the agenda.

This is one of those moments with Mox and Ronni that bridges the difference between her serious planner girlie self, and his laid back and relaxed type. They're such polar opposites on paper, but the chemistry is palpable. I adore this couple so much! I love how seriously unserious he is, and how she's driven to absolute distraction by his chaos. On the flip side, I love how she can keep him grounded, but also still relax and meet him in the middle.

Let's get snowed in with Elliot and Ronni.

Love,

Eden

Chapter One

Elliot

Dating a Type-A Planner Girly is fucking hard.

After all I've put Ronni through this season, the least I could do is pamper her a little bit. Dealing with the stress of my ex, the press, and anything head office can dream up, she should have cracked under the pressure; hell, I'm close to it myself. A getaway weekend where neither of us talk about hockey, schedules, routines, events, or press; sounds simple enough, right?

Wrong.

Staring at the email on my phone for the last ten minutes hasn't changed a damn thing about it. Promo filming at practice with sponsors in two weeks as a team, right over the reservations that I set at Nico's. Groaning, I drop my head back on my shoulders.

"Fuck my life," I mutter, as I lean back farther and my head makes contact with the polished wood panel with an audible *thunk*. Just for good measure, I do it again. *Thunk.*

"What's up? You look like you're trying to do calculus in your head," Bishop asks from beside me, throwing his massive legs across the bench. He settles beside me, his giant arms crossed against his chest, and waits quietly for me to get my words out. That's the best part of him: he doesn't make me talk, and he listens to my dumbass ideas.

"I'm trying to actually plan a date. A real one. We never get to go do anything, and I want to fix that. I got us reservations at Nico's, but just got an email that I'm tied up with events that day instead. And they were booked months out so it could be the offseason before I get another one."

"Aw, honey, you tried!" Bishop says mockingly, batting his eyelashes at me. "And I thought you didn't love me."

"Not for you, fucker," I grouse, shoving at him. "It's for Ronni. I just want to spend time with her where she doesn't have to plan anything and it doesn't become a total disaster."

"And Nico's was the best you could come up with for that? Really, dude? Why not just invite Robicheaux and Kozlov along, too. You can make it a double date."

I freeze. He has a point. Nico's is the team favorite hangout, really, mostly because of their commitment to our privacy. Also, they have amazing food. Maybe he is right, and it is the easy way out. "I guess I could do something better..." I trail off, trying to think of what, if anything, we can do instead.

"Do you need a hand, rookie?" The insult stings; just because I'm not good at the date planning thing, doesn't mean I don't have experience. And just because he has a solid eight years on me doesn't mean he was always the veteran. Although, maybe he's right this time; maybe I am making a rookie mistake.

"Maybe."

"Look," he says, pulling out his phone. "Call this guy. He takes care of my hideout. It's where I spend the offseason, but it has all you two need for a weekend away. Hot tub, views for days, massive kitchen, tons of privacy. You don't even have to leave the property. Just don't break the headboard, okay? It's custom and took a year for me to get it installed. Oh. And certain doors are locked for a reason. Don't go in there. Cool?"

"Oh, yeah, that would be sweet! Thanks, Val. I really mean it."

"It's nothing. It sits empty most of the year, anyway. You crazy kids have some fun, okay? Don't do anything I wouldn't do."

"Yes, Dad, we'll be home before curfew, too," I laugh.

With another curse and a shove, he gets up and leaves me alone with my thoughts. I make the call like he suggested, making sure that everything would work out, what time frame I would be on, and preparing the menu. Thankfully, eating like Bishop means that he knows how to stock the kitchen for me, too. Now to just figure out Ronni's schedule and make sure we can get away.

"Moxley! Are you coming to practice or not?" Coach's words echo off the walls. Cursing, I put my phone back in my locker and walk to the rink.

Even while skating laps, I feel like maybe this could be the best mistake to ever happen. She's going to love it. I think. Or hope. Man, I hope we don't get snowed in for a week if she hates it...

Chapter Two

Ronni

Elliot is acting really strange. Like, not his usual brand of strange—because let's face it, he is, to a degree—but he's acting even stranger than that. Maybe not goalie-level strange, because that's honestly in a category all by itself, but still, this is more than normal. It's like he's keeping a secret. I don't know if he's aware yet, but he has zero poker face, and it's super easy to read him if he's hiding anything. Whatever it is, he's doing a crappy job of hiding it and completely not answering me when I ask directly.

He asked Jess about my schedule this week, even though I've had nothing new added for this month and he could have just asked me directly. He seemed focused on this coming weekend for some reason. The only thing on my schedule this weekend is hopefully keeping a certain hockey player out of the gossip news cycle for once.

Ever since we started dating, we've been trying to walk this fine line between being open about our dating, and not. It's not like he's hiding us; everyone we work with directly knows that we've gotten close. Head office doesn't know exactly how close, or the press, and that's where we don't want to end up. It's still pretty new and fresh, and we'd like to see where we end up in a few months first before we get HR involved.

However, at the rate he's going, everyone is going to know everything and I'll need to smother him with a pillow. Pity, really; he's the first real boyfriend I've had in a long time who can think about someone other than themselves.

I watch him across the press room, giving a couple final statements to a newer reporter. As everyone starts to file out, I jerk my head toward the hallway, silently relaying to him that I need to talk to him. In true Elliot fashion, he says goodbye to the reporter and jogs my way with a grin.

"What's up, Snow Queen?" he says, reaching past me to push the door open. And they say chivalry is dead. Smiling in thanks, I pass through before he follows me into the hall.

"I just had some last minute things to go over with you, if you're free for a few minutes." I watch with a grin as he jogs up, the toggles on his hoodie strings clicking together. His woodsy cologne hits me, and it's like a soft caress. We're walking an appropriate, professional distance apart, but that scent reminds me of all the times he's been a lot closer than that.

"Absolutely! I am all yours! You know that, right?" He winks, and on anyone else the line would have been cheesy, but from him, I can't help but smile in return.

"Let's go in here." I point to an empty conference room ahead of us.

"Sure thing." He jogs ahead to open the door again. I really do need to thank his mother for his impeccable manners. I walk in ahead of him, tripping the sensor for the lights, and wait as he closes the door behind us. I hear the latch click into place, and I whirl on him, nearly jumping out of my own skin when I realize he's moved farther into the room as well, and is now three inches away.

"You wanted to—woah. Are you mad at me?" His hands instinctively grasp my hips, steadying me before I fall. "What's wrong? Why are you mad?"

"What have you been up to?" I ask, trying to keep it casual, but I can hear the sharp tone to my question. He'll forgive me for it; he always does. I'm just intense like that.

"Practices have run long this week, and I was a little late to the presser because Bishop was hogging the shower today, but I apologized before I started answering questions! Was it not enough? I can write a statement."

"That's not it, Elliot. Why are you asking Jess questions about my schedule?"

"Your schedule? What...oh. That." His lips press together in a tight, white line, like he's trying to keep the words from spilling out.

Stay calm, Ronni, he probably has a good reason for all of this. I take a calming breath before asking again, "You're getting it. What have you been up to?"

It should be comical to watch a fully grown, six-foot-four giant of a man shaking his head "no" while clamping his mouth shut. I should be laughing at this, but I frankly just cannot deal with it anymore.

"Spill it, Moxley," I bark at him. "What is going through that thick skull of yours?"

Chapter Three

Elliot

I'm not ready to tell her everything yet, but with the way she's standing there, staring me down and tapping her heel, I know that if I don't say something soon, she's going to gut me with my own skate blade.

"Babe, give me a minute—"

"Don't you 'babe' me, Elliot. Why are you asking everyone about minute details about me instead of asking me about it?"

"It's supposed to be a surprise," I grumble, stuffing my sweaty hair back out of my face again.

"Oh!" She freezes, the surprise etched all over her face. "Oh, that's sweet, but I don't surprise well."

"I noticed," I mutter with a frown.

"So," she starts, stepping closer to me, her hands sliding up my lapels to my tie which she fiddles with. I knew it wasn't quite centered, it felt off. "What was this surprise you had planned for me?"

"I know someone who has a cabin over in the mountains. I wanted to take you on a weekend getaway. Just you, me, a professional grade kitchen, a crackling fire, a hot tub..." My brain short circuits as her hands reach my collar and she starts fiddling with the hairs on the back of my neck.

Don't get hard at the arena, don't get hard at the arena, Don't. Get. Hard. At. The. Arena!

"El? I like this surprise." She pops up on her toes to leave me with a scorching kiss, before walking off as though nothing had happened. "Let me know what I need to pack!"

That woman is going to kill me, and I'm probably going to be grateful for it.

Chapter Four

Ronni

I have to give Elliot credit: when he goes big with something, he goes Big. Capital B.

The drive up was peaceful, and the view here left me speechless. Now, sitting on the sofa staring out the floor-to-ceiling windows at the evergreens below, basking in the warmth of the fire that was already crackling cheerily when we arrived, I wonder if we even need to go back to civilization. Granted, the nearest grocery is an hour away, and there had been warning signs about rock slides and treacherous winter driving conditions; I don't think I would like it so much then. But for now? I'm in love with a cabin. Maybe not "write a romance novella about being in love with a sentient being" love, but I could be very happy staying here for long periods of time. If the internet was solid, I could totally make an appeal to work remotely.

"Need a refill?" Elliot calls over from the kitchen. I glance at my half-full wine glass and the charcuterie he made me for a snack. I'm under strict orders to sit and relax, and not think or do anything hockey-related, except for him. As if I could ever not think of him, honestly.

"I could use a little bit, maybe. Are you coming back over here? I'm lonely." After popping around the corner with the chilled bottle in hand, he focuses on filling my glass. I can't help but grin at him wearing a "Kiss the Cook" apron over his jeans and t-shirt.

"In a minute. I need to get the rest of dinner in the oven before we starve." He leans over the arm of the couch, kissing me softly before heading back to the kitchen.

Sighing, I pull out my phone. Signal up here is spotty at best, but I have enough bars to get more e-books downloaded, and a couple texts with Jess.

Jess: I'm so glad you made it! And yes, everything is fine here before you ask.

Me: Good. I know it's only a few days but anything can happen!

Jess: Just relax and enjoy that man and the view—or both at the same time!

She has a point. I settle back under the wool blanket and open a new book, looking out the window one more time before I fall into the text.

That view. I can only imagine how beautiful it is with snowfall. It has to look like a postcard; white clumps resting on the evergreen and watching the snowflakes dance before the windows must be breathtaking. The weather report said there was a chance of snow. Closing my eyes briefly, I send up a small wish that I can see that happen just once before we go home.

Chapter Five

Elliot

There's some quote about best laid plans, and mice and men. Something like that. Also, that the path to hell is paved with the bricks of good intentions. Welcome to my road. I built it myself.

I wake up before Ronni, planning to make breakfast and deliver it to her in bed. No, really; waffles with fresh strawberries and whipped cream, and a perfect wake up call. Instead, I have to figure out how to tell her that it snowed last night.

Not just a little dusting of snow, but like a foot. Snowmageddon happened. Bishop had tried to blow up my phone last night to get us into town, but we were, as usual, busy. We might be able to get back down in about a week, depending on how long it takes to clear the pass.

She's going to freak the hell out and I can't do anything about it.

"El? Are you out here?"

Jumping, I look down the hall at our bedroom, knowing she will be out here in a matter of moments. "In the kitchen, babe," I call out, bracing myself for her to come past the windows and—

"Oh wow! Did you see the view? I didn't know it was going to snow so much last night! It's beautiful!"

I cringe, wondering if I tell her now that our well-planned trip just took a spur-of-the-moment change in plans. Moving things away from the heat, I walk into the living room where she stopped.

"About that, babe..." The words get stuck in my throat and I just can't break this moment for her. She's practically pressed against the glass, the heat from her hands and breath steaming up the windows where she stands. Her socked feet are hopping back and forth, like the excitement in her is too much to keep still. If I tell her I knew it was a possibility, she'll be heartbroken. It would have diverted us from the black and white "Plan" and put us on a path of spontaneous actions that she isn't usually a fan of. I can't ruin this for her. I'll tell her later, I convince myself.

"I have breakfast ready if you want some," I say instead.

"That's awesome, thanks, El!" Her words fog up the glass more, and I watch her reach up to draw "EM + VS" in the remnants before it resumes the view outside.

"I'll bring it out to the couch, babe, okay?"

"Yes, please!"

Well, if nothing else, she seems happy with this so far.

Chapter Six

Ronni

Another snowy morning at our winter wonderland cabin! I wake up more refreshed than I probably have in years, with Elliot snuggled up against me, keeping me warm. It is absolute perfection and I never want this to end. I slide out of bed, careful not to wake him so I can make us breakfast. It is the least I can do!

Perhaps going wireless is something we need to do more often, I think as I throw together my yoga pants and over-sized sweater. The view is gorgeous, evergreen trees as far as the eye can see.

The coffee begins to percolate, and I hum contentedly to myself. The combination of richness from the brew and the warm spices from the cinnamon rolls, combined with the crisp smell of snow on the air, puts a smile on my face. I am in a cozy little bubble and nothing can bring me down. Not even the incoming snowstorm.

I don't think Elliot knows that I know. Honestly, he shouldn't be surprised that I scanned the forecast before we left town. I have always planned everything down to the minute, but this time, I opted to see what happens if I let go.

I can trust him, I do, but sometimes it's just so hard to let go of the details.

Every now and then I catch him looking at me with that forehead wrinkle and wonder if this is the time he'll say something, and instead he pours on the charm and surprises me with another activity for us to do.

Chapter Seven

Elliot

I'll admit that I'm a coward. I've had two days now to tell her that not only are we at the mercy of the road conditions to get out, but there was a decent chance I should have called this whole thing off before we ever left the city.

Yeah, I heard that there "might" be snow in the forecast. How was I supposed to know that when they say snow here, they mean it! The weatherman is usually wrong in our area!

The guilt gnaws at my gut, especially as I watch her pull out the hot spot and laptop for this afternoon, trying to get enough signal to get her emails to load. I managed to get a call out to Bishop's property owner, who said that there was a chance for tomorrow if nothing acts up, but there's no promises.

Technically, we should have been home by now. I didn't intend for us to get stuck up here. I'm just glad there's more than enough food for us to stay longer! Taking stock of the perishables and the pantry, we'll be okay for a few more days, easily. This just wasn't what I envisioned for our romantic getaway cabin.

She doesn't seem upset with me, and the conversations we have had over the last couple days have been great for us and our new relationship. We have cuddled, talked about plans for the future, shared little tidbits from college, and it's been great. Going to sleep beside her is amazing, and I wonder if the team will really freak out when I quit sharing with Bishop and instead just get a suite for me and Ronni.

This could have gone so much worse, but I'm happy with it anyway.

\#

I'm in love with a card shark.

She's grinning at me over the top of her cards and a fat stack of candy. What started as just a friendly game of poker turned into her fleecing me for all of my candy bars.

"All in," I say as I shove the last of my snack hoard toward the middle of the coffee table.

"All in? Are you sure about that?" Her eyes, wide and innocent, give away nothing. What have I gotten myself into?

"Absolutely." Flipping my cards over, I smirk. There's no way she can beat my hand unless she has...

"Oh, sorry about that," she coos, raking her winnings over to her side of the table.

"You're not the least bit sorry," I dig back, getting up from the floor. "I'm getting more snacks, do you want anything?"

"I think I'm good for a bit."

I wander around the kitchen, foraging for snacks, when I realize that I need to still talk to her. I will. I will totally do that. Gathering everything, I walk back out prepared to open my own stupid mouth and say something when—

"We should play a game," she proposes, gathering up the cards and the candy bars.

"What else is there to play?" I put down the food on the cleared table, then settle myself onto the couch beside her again.

She turns, eyeballing me. I'm attempting to look calm, relaxed, but I feel anything but. I can feel my knee start to bounce, and I shift my position in an attempt to hide the motion. Her gaze lifts from that knee and I know she knows.

"We should play Truth or Dare."

Chapter Eight

Ronni

"We should play Truth or Dare."

I definitely did not expect those words to fall out of my mouth, but here we are, stretched out on the large couch, and the gauntlet has been thrown.

"Truth or Dare? Like, the game Sami used to play with her little friends at sleepovers? I'm pretty sure that was embarrassing for all parties involved."

"Why not? I mean, it could be a way to learn more about each other. Anyway, do you have anything else planned for the rest of the night?"

"Actually," he starts off, leaning over me, "I have a few ideas."

"Later, it's comfortable here."

He laughs, and settles back into the couch. "Okay, let's start. Truth or dare, Ronni?"

I tuck my legs under me, settling in for the long haul. "Truth."

"Tell me when you first started to not think of me as another dumb jock."

Oh, he's swinging for the fences. I think over my answer. "Remember when you ran all the way to the locker room to get me your extra game jersey because it was the only spare shirt you had?" Grinning, he nods. "Pretty sure that was it."

"That was the day I'm pretty sure I saw my future with you. Seeing you in my jersey did things for me." Clearing his throat, he utters a single word. "Dare."

"Dare?" Cocking my head at him, I wonder what I can get him to do within the confines of the cabin.

"I'm not afraid or ashamed of anything you can make me do, Snow Queen."

"I dare you to read one of my books."

"You want me to read a book?" Shrugging his shoulders, he holds out his hands for my tablet. "Pick one."

I hand him my tablet and listen as he starts narrating a passage that I had just read earlier. Grinning, I watch as his eyebrows raise higher and higher as he reads spicier and spicier content, interjecting commentary as he goes.

"Wait, you actually like this?" He taps the screen twice more. "Would—" His voice cracks, and he coughs. "Would you like me to try this sometime?"

"Maybe," I say noncommittally, waiting to receive my tablet back. "Book boyfriends are different."

"I can tell. Kind of impressed, I didn't know anyone could bend that way."

Settling back into our spots on the couch, I consider my options. While I trust Elliot to an extent, I don't know if I trust him to not pull a prank like he does with the players. Playing it safe, I say, "Truth."

"Tell me about Ronni as a child. What were you like? Did you have a huge color-coded planner when you were twelve?"

"I did not, actually, I didn't learn to do color coding

until high school. It kept my assignments straight. Twelve-year-old me," I pause, "she thought she wanted to play a sport, but actually wasn't good at it. I was better on the sideline, keeping stats and tracking paperwork, even then. It's like I was built to get into sports behind the scenes." He smiles and I can tell he's trying to imagine a younger version of me, riding the bench beside a coach, waving a clipboard around. "I didn't mind, really, and when my friends moved up in leagues and needed help keeping things together, I was their go-to person. I guess it just came naturally to me." I smile at the nostalgia. "So what's it going to be, Elliot? Truth or Dare?"

"Truth," he says, a cocky smirk on his face.

He has no idea what's about to hit him. Grinning, I slide closer, straddling his lap so we're face to face. My fingers slide through his wavy hair, and I get butterflies when his eyelids flutter shut.

"When were you going to tell me that you knew we'd get snowed in?"

He goes rigid, his grin falling slowly, and his eyes wide. Like a deer in the headlights.

"You knew?" His question is soft, disbelief clear in his tone. I nod lightly. "You knew the whole time?"

I give him a soft smile. "Of course I did. I saw the weather reports before we left town."

"And you still came? I mean, you could have told me no."

"I could have. But I didn't." I shrug. "When was the last time we took any serious time to ourselves?" I struggle to remember myself. In the offseason? Maybe? "I think we're long overdue for a break, and to be honest, it sounded great. Relaxing in a cabin with minimal connection to the outside world? Just you and me, with no deadlines?"

"And," he pauses, chewing on his lip the way he does when he's thinking. "And you're not mad about it?"

"Heavens, no," I say on a laugh. " Why would I be mad about it? This has been a great break away from the arena. It couldn't have been better if I had planned it myself."

He stares at me, awestruck, his hands shifting restlessly along my sides. "You beautiful, ridiculously smart woman."

I grin at him, giggling. "Are you mad I kept it from you?"

His head shifts slowly to the left and right, his eyes never leaving my face.

"God, I love you," he whispers, barely on a breath. "Come here."

He takes my head between his hands and pulls me closer for a kiss. It's soft and sweet to start with, one he's given me a hundred times, but with a soft hum, he deepens it; hungrier, hotter, as his teeth nip at my bottom lip. His heartbeat under my palm is fast, and I can't help but notice that I feel my own in sync against my ribcage. Our connection is so strong.

His hands tuck under my thighs and with a squeak from me, he's standing, holding me up. In a matter of strides he has us up the stairs and in the bedroom, stretched across the large bed. His weight presses me into the soft blankets as a hand slides restlessly from my knee—hooking my leg around his back—up my hip, around the curve of my breast and back again.

"What am I going to do with you," he murmurs against my lips, pressing his hips into mine on a slow grind before trailing kisses down the column of my neck. "I have you here for the next two days, easily. Should I keep you right here?" He grinds again. "Should I punish you for keeping secrets?" He nips at my collarbone. "Naughty girl."

I gasp at the soft sting, sighing as he places a kiss over

the light hurt. His playful side makes me smile, but I know this won't last long. He can never keep up the short and sweet foreplay. My hand slides into his hair, drawing a growly moan from him in return.

Sitting up some, he grasps the bottom of my shirt, whipping it over my head quickly. He freezes, looking at the pale pink bralette that I bought specifically for our trip. A smirk turns up the corner of his mouth, popping his dimple that I adore so much.

"Little tease." Fingertips trace the edges, his eyes wide and awestruck. "You had this in your bag the entire time, didn't you?" A single fingertip traces lower, circling my belly button. "And," he trails down to the waistband of my leggings, "is it a matching set?"

I nod my head a little, my teeth digging into my bottom lip as I watch on. In a smooth shift, he pulls my leggings down and off my legs, leaving me in the scraps of lace. "You like it?" The question I ask is soft, barely a whisper.

"Oh, I love it, Snow Queen," he responds, sliding his fingertips over the textured material. "It's almost a shame to take it off. Or cover it. Both, yeah, both."

"Later," I almost beg.

Chapter Nine

Elliot

My Snow Queen is full of surprises today.

Watching her take over is beautiful. Sure, she's almost always in charge at work, but to watch her like this, fully in her element and taking what pleases her, is just beautiful. I don't have the words to tell her how beautiful she is, and that I would willingly let her do whatever she fucking wants to me.

I need to relax, I tell myself, *before I ruin this for both of us.* I try slowly breathing in and out, reciting NHL teams in alphabetical order, something has to work. Watching her slide my sweats off slowly, deliberately, I take in everything about her. Her focus, eyes locked on mine as she crawls back up onto the bed, prowling over my prone form. What is that saying, turnabout is fair play? I think that's what we have here.

Her soft mouth presses a warm kiss to my length and I grit my teeth against the urge to thrust my hips forward into the touch. She giggles softly, placing a kiss against the flared head before climbing upward. Oh, my queen isn't in the mood to play today. I'm good with that. *Yeah, I'm totally good with that,* I think as she straddles my thighs, leaning forward to kiss me again.

Settling her hips into mine, my hands grab at her butt, holding her still, just so we can enjoy this one moment. Our eyes lock and I hiss in pleasure as she sinks lower onto me. Her hips shift slightly, finding a better angle for her, and my eyes roll back in my head. She's going to be the death of me.

"My turn," I gasp, flipping us so I take the dominant position again. Driving myself into her, I can feel myself drawing up. I won't last long, but I couldn't slow down now if I tried. "Driving me crazy with those little scraps, you knew what you were doing, didn't you?" I growl the question, sliding my thumb across her sensitive nub. "What else are you hiding in that bag of yours? Hmm?"

She moans loudly, her short fingernails scraping up my chest. Damnit, she knows all the right buttons to push. I feel myself lose the rhythm but it can't be helped, she's clenching around me and her nails are biting into my back and I just let go.

My breath escapes me and I see stars, feeling like I'm just on the edge of passing out. I love that floaty feeling, and I know she does, too, as I look down at her dreamy expression.

"You did that on purpose," I accuse without heat as I lean down, kissing her softly.

"Hmm, maybe," she hums happily, a smug look on her face.

"Feel better?"

"Immensely."

Chapter Ten

Ronni

There's someone—or something—outside the house.

"Elliot?" I whisper. "Are you awake?" He hums in his sleep before his breath resettles. "Elliot. There's someone outside." I nudge his arm at my waist, hoping that poking him will wake him up. Nothing. "Moxley," I say louder. Still nothing. I inhale deeply, test which if my nails is sharpest against my palm, and then poke him. Hard.

"SHIT! I'm awake, Coach, I—" He looks around the room. "Ronni? You up, babe?"

"There's someone outside. I heard something."

He moves with a quickness, assuming some kind of fighting pose in the middle of the bedroom wearing nothing. As he stills, I can hear it again: scraping noises.

"Stay put. Close the door behind me and only open it if you hear me," he orders as he throws on a pair of jeans and heads into the darkened hall.

I curl into a ball under the quilts, shivering. It will be okay, I'm sure of it. Glancing at my phone on the nightstand, I notice that it's just before sunup. I hear Elliot's voice, and slam my eyes shut. *Please don't let us die on a mountain where no one will find us.*

"Babe? It's okay," Elliot yells into the house. "They got the plow up to the house. It's a clear drive all the way home if we want to go today." As fast as my heart soared at the "drive home" part, it fell just as hard at the "we can go today." I don't know if I even do want to go home today. I'm trying to decide how to tell him this when he throws the door wide and pops around the doorframe. "Babe?"

"I heard, that's great," I say, smiling at him.

His head tilts, like those golden retriever puppies. "You don't sound happy about it. Are you okay? We don't have to go right away unless you want to, but fair warning, you only have like, another two cups' worth of your creamer left. Two more coffee cups and then you're down to regular milk, and I know you hate it when that happens."

"I know, and it's probably a good thing, it's just..." I sigh, trying to put my words together in my head. "I guess I kind of got used to being here with you and I'm going to miss it."

"So what you're saying is we should do this again sometime?"

"Yeah, I think so," I say, moving over on the bed to let him in. His cool skin wrapping around me gives me goose-bumps. "Maybe when it's warmer out, so we don't get snowed in every time, okay?"

"Deal. God I love you," he whispers against my neck, holding me closer and taking in my warmth. "So, how about we go back to sleep for a little bit, and then take our time going back home? No rush to get down the mountain."

"Hey, El?"

"Yeah, Babe."

"What if we don't go back to sleep?"

He never has to use words to say what he feels about that idea.

Chapter Eleven

Elliot

Coming back to the arena always feels like coming home, but this time it has a bittersweet edge I can't quite place my finger on.

Did I miss my routine, practices, and workouts? Absolutely.

Did I miss hanging out with Bishop in the locker room? Damn straight.

But...do I now miss the little things like snuggling on the couch with Ronni and just watching the snow falling outside? More than my heart can bear.

Which is probably why I'm cruising real estate listings in the same area as Bishop's cabin instead of paying attention to the game tapes. Normally I'm absolutely all about watching tapes, finding out where their goalies' weak sides are, who gasses out faster, who is a real threat on goal. Today, I can't be bothered. I can't focus. All I can see or envision is getting us our own cabin, with our own view, and making all new memories all over our own place.

I can feel the corners of my mouth turn up as I look

down at my screen at a similar setup that is supposed to be ten minutes down the road from Bishop. Close enough we could hang out in the off season if we want to, but far enough away we both have our privacy. The realtor is anxious to talk, and I'm already working out my schedule for when I can go over. And absolutely, I will let Ronni know and not leave this as a last-minute surprise for her.

After all: It is for her. It's for us. I can see us spending off-seasons here, bringing Gabby and Sami in between treatments for a getaway, sending Ronni and Jess up for girls' weekends. It is absolute perfection, and damnit, it will be ours.

"Moxley!" Coach's loud voice makes me jump, dropping my phone onto the short carpet below. "Get your ass off the porn sites and pay fucking attention!"

"Shit," I curse under my breath. "Sorry, Coach," I call out, before bending down to brush my fingers against empty carpet. *Where did it go?*

"Here you go," Bishop whispers, handing me my phone. "Quit being so damned obvious. She's not going to sell that property to anyone except for you, trust me."

"I know, but I don't want to leave anything to chance. I need a plan B just in case."

"You don't need a plan B, you need patience. Chill the fuck out, Mox."

I sink lower in my seat, my right knee bouncing as I continue watching and listening to the coaching commentary. Bishop is right, there will be time afterward to get this straightened out.

* * *

Three months later...

"Elliot, I already know what the place looks like, isn't this a bit much?" Ronni's laugh is infectious, but I am standing firm. I love surprises. I want to see her eyes light up when we walk into our cabin and see our things for the first time. I check the blindfold one more time. We're at the last pull-off before our place.

"I still want to see you surprised," I counter. "It's my favorite part."

"Okay, fine, I'll play along." She rests her head back on the headrest, her hands folded on her denim covered thighs. "Just give me a heads up before we walk. I don't want to fall."

"I'll never let you fall, Snow Queen," I promise, pulling back onto the rough pavement.

The view is exactly how I remembered it from the listing. The large wraparound porch beckoning us closer, the rich wood seasoned by the sun and weather. The bright red door was cheery, and if I was honest, it was the part that jumped out at me. It reminded me of Ronni. Putting the car in park again, I turn off the ignition.

"We're here? Is it time? Can I take it off now?"

"Shh, let me come around and open the door for you."

She huffs, but stays still. I hop out and race around the car, breathing in that fresh green smell of trees and new growth, the fresh dirt. I open her door and wait for her to hold out her hand to me. It's a practiced movement, and I love the sparks that go up my arm taking her hand every single time; this time is no different. Her fingertips sliding along my slightly calloused ones, soft on rough, give me a shiver.

Ronni carefully stands upright, a real feat with her vision gone, and gives me her other hand for guidance.

"Here, let me do this," I say, sliding one arm behind her and picking her up bridal style.

"Elliot!" She squeals in surprise, but wraps her arms around my neck all the same.

"I've got you," I assure her, carrying her the three steps up onto the porch. "Here we go," I add, setting her feet down on our welcome mat.

"Can I..." she trails off, motioning to the blindfold.

"Let me," I murmur, sliding my fingers along her cheeks,lifting the material with it. Her eyes are clamped closed, and I see her jolt at the light on her eyelids. Slowly she flutters her eyes open, taking everything around us into focus.

"Oh. Oh, Elliot, this is..."

"It's down the road from Bishop's, actually."

Her sneakers make a soft shuffling sound as she turns slowly, looking off the porch and into the trees. Her gasps of surprise as she takes in every detail, running her fingers along the rough-hewn railing, makes my heart flip.

"Oh, Elliot, it's beautiful," her hushed voice trails off as she approaches the door again. "Can we..."

"Go in? It's ours, Snow Queen, we can do whatever we want with it." Reaching into my pocket, I pull out a single silver key on a keychain showing our Ice Wolves mascot in full hockey gear. She takes it with a grin and presses it into the lock. With a slight shove, the door opens into our open concept cabin.

Her hand trails along the back of the couch and the fleece throw blanket tossed over it. Grinning, she walks across to the floor to ceiling windows, looking out into the valley; the same valley she looked at months ago.

"And it's all ours?"

"Until you don't want it anymore."

"Never. I'm never getting rid of this. I love it here. I can't wait to make new memories with you here."

"Let's start this weekend," I offer, shooting her a cocky grin. She returns my look and runs toward me, expecting me to catch her; as always I do.

I can't wait to get snowed in with her again.

K.R. Orinick - Melodye Davis - Emily Michel -
Clint Baker - Helga R. Paxton - Lee VanBeek -
Eden Knox - Ivy M. Young - Krys Strong -
Corin Dively

TATTOOED WINGS & STRANGER THINGS

A Fairy Godmother Anthology

Introduction

Some people may tell you I have a slight obsession with charity anthologies.

They're not totally wrong. At one point I had something like 4 anthology submissions rolling at the same time, for separate groups and charities, all with timelines due within about a 4 month period. I couldn't say no, they all meant too much to me. That's how "Fairy Godfather" came to be part of a sweet little anthology called "Tattooed Wings & Stranger Things."

Tattooed was a project near and dear to my heart, and came about while a good friend was struggling with cancer. Royalties from the collection went to the American Cancer Society while in print, with rights reverting back to the authors afterward.

This short does not follow in the spicy footsteps of it's predecessors, which all took a very strong dive into spicy territory. This one stays at a solid PG rating, with just some slight obscenities from Elliot and Ronni. It was my first attempt at dipping my toes into "green pepper" territory, or slightly on the outskirts of romance. The romantic relationship here exists prior to chapter 1, in "Tripping for Number 68." If you haven't read that one yet, that gives you more insight into Elliot and Ronni's relationship.

In the "Tripping" timeline, this falls midway into the book. Shortly after they start their relationship, but before the third act breakup. Between chapters 17 and 18 would be a good spot to place this one, I think. Their relationship status is still tentative, and she still struggles with being aggravated at his chaotic "heart of gold" tendencies. If you want to stay in chronological order, pause now and start Tripping, pause at the end of 17, read this through to the end of chapter 5, but stop before the epilogue.

I hope this little snapshot into the Ice Wolves and their off-ice shenanigans is a fun and fluffy little side quest that cements Elliot's cinnamon roll status.

Chapter One

In the beginning, there was a jersey.

"Veronica Snow?" The male voice asked after a tentative knock on her office door, a bright yellow padded sleeve in one hand.

"That's me, come on in." Veronica "Ronni" Snow waved him in. She opened the package while he pulled up the information on his handheld device. "I didn't order this," she told him, as he held the screen toward her for a signature.

"The invoice has your name on it. And so does the sticker." He wasn't wrong. The label was specific to her attention.

"Right, but I didn't order a–" she paused as she finished pulling out the item. "A youth large jersey?"

She looked down at the small jersey; the Ice Pups logo for the Mites team stitched instead of the Ice Wolves. White tackle twill embroidered patches were sewn precisely onto the "home game" blue jersey with the navy back shadow and white stripes. The name and number on the back wasn't Moxley's 68, so maybe it wasn't for his niece

Gabby, either. The numbers, big white blocks declaring its wearer to be number 36, belonged to Valentin Bishop on the Ice Wolves. This jersey, however, said player 36 was a... Callahan? The name wasn't familiar to her.

"I'm just following instructions, ma'am," he replied.

"Fine, I'll work it out. Thanks."

It couldn't be a Make-a-Wish situation, she would have known. If they didn't go through her office for organizing the team visit, then they would have gone through Jess first, who would have coordinated schedules with her as well. She thought about dropping a quick email to her friend and former officemate to confirm anyway, though.

Ronni wondered if maybe the skate shop made a clerical error by sending it up to her new office instead of Team Relations. With a shrug of her shoulders, she sat the jersey on the sideboard, intending to take it down to the shop later so it could go to its rightful owner.

However, time got away between one PR disaster and another, and days later, the jersey still sat in her office. Each morning she swore she would take it downstairs where it belonged until work got in the way. Tomorrow, she swore one last time as she locked up her office for the night.

Chapter Two

Next came the skates.

The sleek black box, emblazoned with the high-end skate brand that Elliot and Bishop especially both favored, gleamed on her coffee table. The blades looked freshly sharpened, ready for game play. Curiouser and curiouser, she thought as she rearranged the items; the jersey laying smoothly on top of the box.

A phone call would fix this, surely. She quickly called her friend Jess in their old office.

"That name sounds kind of familiar, but I can't quite place it," Jess said, clicking on her keyboard on the other end of the phone. "That name isn't showing up on any of the rosters I have. Sorry, Ronni."

"I'm sure there's a logical reason, but I thought I would start with you first in case it was forwarding the PR things to me."

Making a mental note to take the skates with the jersey later, she went on about her fully scheduled day.

Then the next day there was the box of performance moisture-wicking tees and leggings arrived with several pairs of socks, clearly intended to fit whoever belonged to the jersey. They all proudly bore the logos of the same brands Elliot favored, just smaller than what he regularly wore on his 6-foot-4 frame. These also arrived with Rockville Ice Pups logos on the left-hand side, and the same "Callahan" last name and block number 36 printed as well.

This time, she walked down to the skate shop and enquired about the mystery deliveries. Johan was out for the day, and no one in the building knew anything outside of what the system said. The order forms were specific: exact brands and sizes to be delivered to Ronni Snow's office. They paid in cash, so card numbers and names weren't available either. No one working at the moment remembered taking the order. Slightly frustrated, and with more questions than she had answers, Ronni returned to her office to ponder over this mystery some more.

On the next day came the gloves. They were the same brand and model as Moxley's regular equipment, supple black leather over padding that gleamed in the overhead lighting. The only difference between Elliot's and this pair is that his personal pair would dwarf her hands, and she could almost get away with wearing these. He'd never fit into a youth medium. She sat them with the jersey and skates, promising to make a trip down to the team shop after her meeting with the Ice Wolves Foundation board of trustees.

Ronni had had enough. She picked up her cell, pulling up Elliot's information and called, listening as the phone rang once. Then again.

"Hey, Snow Queen," his voice murmured.

"Hey yourself," she returned. "I have a question for you."

"I'm all yours, babe. What's up?"

"Why am I collecting Mites gear in my office?"

He stayed silent for a few beats before cursing. "One moment," he said, before saying something to his party and then walking to a quieter area. "Ronni, I can explain…"

"Don't you 'Ronni' me," she broke in. "Why am I getting tiny versions of your equipment in my office? It's looking like a locker room here! I can't work in these conditions!"

"I know, I know, but there's a really good reason. I promise."

"Oh really? Tell me."

"I can't yet. Not here anyway. Just," he sighed. "Can you set them aside somewhere? They don't need to leave the arena yet, but I can't be seen with them anywhere else. Just trust me?"

"This makes no sense, Mox."

"It will. I just need you to hold on to them for a few more days. Just until I come back off the road. I promise. I can explain over coffee when I get back to the arena."

"Fine," she grumbled. "I have some space in my extra filing cabinet. They can stay there for now. But I want answers from you, Moxley. I mean it."

"You're the best, Snow Queen!"

Clearly, that agent of chaos that she tolerated was involved somehow, but she had to wait on him to explain this.

Chapter Three

By Friday, the filing cabinet was full. So was the closet.

A custom painted goalie helmet had showed up during her afternoon teleconference meeting Wednesday, causing the board members to question if she was okay when she felt her eyes widen. The helmet sat atop the filing cabinet, the blue paint gleaming under the LED's. A slightly smaller version of Val Bishop's own game helmet, with a series of wolves in aggressive poses.

Then came the goalie pads.

The box filled up the space underneath the desktop, leaving Ronni no choice but to sit cross-legged in her chair for the next two days. With each delivery, large or small, Ronni got more and more frustrated. Why couldn't he get these delivered to his apartment like any normal person? Why her office?

And the newest and biggest question: Why goalie gear?

The goalie pads were the final straw for her. She marched down to the locker room, knowing that she would find that ridiculous man that she kind of liked after practice.

Considering he made it home from the road game series yesterday, and did not stop by to see her this afternoon before practice, her frustrations were at an all-time high.

Jean-Luc Robicheaux came out of the door as she approached. He froze with his hand still on the door, before slowly easing his way out into the hallway to face her.

"Hey, Ms. Snow," he greeted, a plastic fake smile on his face. "It's been a minute since you've been down this way, huh?" A nervous hand scratched at the damp hair at his neckline; a definite tell that he was nervous, she knew from his press conferences.

"I know. I usually try to stay away from your area here. You know why I'm down here, right?"

"Looking for Mox?"

She nodded. "Is he still in there?"

"Um..." he slammed his lips shut as she stopped in front of him, arms crossed, heel tapping on the concrete.

"Don't you dare cover for him, Jean-Luc Robicheax, or else. Remember who knows which players enjoy press conferences and those who don't." Her clipped words chilled the surrounding air.

He sighed before giving in, opening the door a crack behind him.

"Boys, get Moxley over here before Ms. Snow comes in." Jeers and laughter erupted from the locker room before he closed the door behind him. "I wouldn't go in there just yet. It's still a mess and the boys haven't dressed out yet. You probably don't want to see what's going on in there."

"Fine. I'll wait right here." She leaned against the wall across from the door. "Go in and tell him to hurry it up because I will come in after him if I think he's wasting my time and hiding."

"Will do, right on it!" With that, he dove back through

the door, pulling it tight behind him. Muffled through the door, she could hear him yell, "Damnit, Mox, she's pissed! She's scary when she's pissed! Please go out there before she comes in here!"

Time slowed to a crawl as she listened to the murmurs behind the door, and the casual conversation and laughs had her jaw clenching in anger. Why was this infuriating man taking so long? With a growl, she pulled out my phone and typed a message to him, angrily stabbing the screen.

"Hey, sorry I took so long, Snow Queen." Her eyes shot up from my screen, locking eyes with him as he slid out of the door, leaning on the wall across from her. "Surprised to see you down here in my hall."

"Yeah, well, I have a problem. Something tells me you know how to fix it."

His spine stiffened. "What's wrong? Can I help?" His brow furrowed a bit. "Who did it? I'll take care of them for you."

"Yeah, actually, you can help, but punching yourself won't fix it. What's with the gear in my office? It looks like the skate shop is using me for an annex."

"Oh yeah. That. I told you I'd take care of it, didn't I?"

"Yeah, but that was three deliveries ago. What is all of this?" He ran a hand through his damp hair, his lips pressed tight. "You could have talked to me, Elliot, you know that."

"I know, it's just–" He cut himself off with a sigh. "I didn't want anyone to know it was me. I wanted to make sure it stayed a surprise."

"Okay," she started. "But how was I supposed to know who they were for? All I know is I have gear coming to my office daily and I can't get into my office now."

"I'm sorry." His mumbled apology hung in the silence between them. "I should've gotten with you sooner."

"So, who needs to get this stuff? I know you have a plan in that thick skull of yours."

"I do, it's just–can we go to your office with this? I really don't want someone to overhear."

She shoved off the wall, walking back in the direction that she had come from originally. After a few steps, she turned, looking back at him.

"Are you coming?" He caught up with her in a few strides, and they continued their walk in silence until she opened her door. Once again, a new box sat on top of her blotter, perfectly centered. "Oh my God, not again!"

"Um, you might not want to open that one."

"And why not?"

Elliot closed the door softly behind him before picking up the brown box. It looked so small in his hands as he took it over to the stack of other boxes.

"It has other gear in it, I promise. You just really don't want to see what else."

She groaned, rolling her head back to stare at the ceiling. "Why, Moxley? Why am I getting miniature gear and why won't you tell me why?"

"Come sit down with me for a minute, okay? I'll explain everything." He settled his tall frame into one chair in front of her desk, and for the sake of neutrality, she sat in the chair beside him. His legs stretched so far that their knees almost touched.

"Okay. Spill it."

He bit his lip, and the knee closest to her bounced. She reached out and settled a hand on the knee, and he picked up her hand to fidget with her fingertips to dispel his nervous energy. "Remember the day when we had that skating event and I took you out on the rink with the kids?" She nodded, a soft smile on her face. "Okay, well, remember the boy that said he couldn't attend camp? Single mom, she could barely afford the practice time?"

"Yeah, you started up the scholarship fund, so she didn't have to. It's covering like 6 other players, too."

"Well, I went to practice the other day, just to interact with the youth players and give a little pep talk. His gear was shot. Nothing was safe, the skates were a size too small. He wasn't safe, babe. I had to help him before he got hurt. If it's that hard to get him into camp, it would be way worse with medical bills."

"So," Ronni started, staring at the boxes. "So you bought him new gear?"

"I can't just outright take someone from the youth league and buy them the things outright. Usually, I'll throw Johan a few bucks here and there to get something small for everyone as they need, but this was way bigger than just an item here or there. He worked with me a little because he had to sharpen his blades, and snuck me into his gear file wish list. "

"Wish list?"

"They check the fitment of gear to make sure that skates are the right size, if helmets fit. They keep a file of what brand and size fit the best. It helps when the parents come in to pick things up or need to budget for replacements."

"Smart thinking," she mused. "So you've been snagging the items off of his list so his mom doesn't have to get it all."

"He wasn't safe, Ronni. Poor fitting skates mean you can't balance or hold yourself right. Not to mention the damage it can do to your feet and ankles. And his helmet? It was falling apart. He's a goalie, that's dangerous. I didn't want him to get hurt and I know what it's like having those gear costs add up."

Ronni leaned against her desk, hand pressed against her

thudding heart. This man, an absolute warrior on ice, railed on and on about gear and unnecessary costs for a family he had no relation to while pacing the carpet before her desk. She couldn't stop the smile creeping onto her face.

"El?" He froze mid-stride, his eyes on her. "I just wish I knew beforehand. We could have done this without turning my office into a storage unit."

"I know," he muttered. "I just thought that if I dropped it off here, no one would connect it to back to me. I just want to surprise him with it and have it stay quiet."

"An anonymous donation."

"Exactly."

"Like a fairy godmother."

His brow wrinkled. "Maybe." His frown deepened. "Not a fairy godmother, just someone who hoped I could have the same help when it was just Ma trying to buy me gear."

"Okay, so how is he going to get his gear now that it's in my office?"

"I didn't work that out exactly ahead of time. I just wanted everything to get here. You're good at that part. How do you think I should do this?"

She looked over the gear and the giant standing in her office.

"Okay, so here are some of my thoughts," she started, circling her desk to sit down in front of her calendar. "You might as well sit down and get comfortable, big guy. This is going to take a minute."

Chapter Four

Ryan gritted his teeth as he crammed his heel down into his skate. He knew he needed a new set;, they were a full size smaller than his school shoes, but it took his mom working two doubles to get those, and the skates...well, they cost a lot more than his shoes.

"Hi, are you Ryan Callahan?" He looked up from the bench to see a red-haired woman standing in the bleachers, wearing an Ice Wolves Athletic Department hoodie.

"Yeah, that's me." She looked a little familiar, but he couldn't place how.

"I know you're due on ice for practice soon, but do you have a second? I need to show you something in the equipment room. Coach said it was okay if I borrowed you."

"Sure, I guess so," he said with shrug.

He stood, grimacing a bit as he settled into the skates before taking a few tentative steps toward the tunnel. She hopped the rail behind him and jogged to catch up.

"Okay, we're just in here," she says, approaching a windowless door with a paper "Private Meeting" sign on the door.

"Mr. Johan has private meetings now?"

"Kind of, Ryan. Let's go in and I can explain more."

"I'm not in trouble, am I? Is my mom in here?"

"You're not in trouble, and yes, she's already in there."

With a sideways glance, he opens the door, seeing his mom sitting on a bench...and nearly walks into the chest of Elliot Moxley, Captain of the Rockville Ice Wolves.

"Um, sorry, sir, I—"

"No, you're fine. Ryan, right?"

The gobsmacked teen just nodded, eyes wide.

"Nice to meet you," Moxley said, holding out his hand. Ryan stared in shock, his own smaller hand raising slowly to slide into his grasp.

"You're—you're...." Ryan's words trailed off.

"Ryan, manners," his mom hinted with a smile. His eyes darted to her, widening in surprise; he clearly could not believe she wasn't as star-struck as he was.

"Come in, sit down for us," Ronni said as she closed the door behind her. "It's okay, Ryan, you aren't in trouble. We just have something we need to show you. Johan, can you help me out?"

"Absolutely, Ronni!" The older man came around the corner to squat before the young boy. "You remember when you came around the shop and we tried on new gear for sizing? And we made notes, right?"

"Yes, sir. You said that they would stay on file for my mom to look at later when," he paused, face screwing up in a frown, glancing at her. "She could look at it later when she was ready."

Elliot threw a glance at Ronni behind Ryan's shoulder, wordlessly saying, "see, I told you." Her face fell as she looked down at the boy.

"Aye, that list. Well, Elliot here saw your list and

wanted to help. So, we have some things over here for you to check out."

"We can come up with the money to pay you back," Ryan's mom says, eyes firm on Elliot.

He just shook his head back. "It was just Ma with me and my sister growing up. I know how hard it was for my mom to cover the gear and camp fees, let alone feeding me after practice. Trust me, it's the least I can do if I can pay it forward to another up-and-coming player. Plus, it's his safety, too. I grew out of gear so fast, it was hard to keep up with. Please, let me help."

Her eyes welled with tears. "It's so much, though…"

"When he turns pro and is making more than he knows what to do with, he'll remember this moment and pass it on. It's the best payback you can give me."

"Mom, look!" Both Elliot and his mom turn to look at Ryan, standing tall in the new skates and gear as he comes around the corner. Tall, proud, confident in his movement.

"Wow," she breathes, looking at him in his new equipment. "How does it feel?"

"The skates feel great, Ma! I can actually move!" He does a little hopping move on the rubberized floor. "Can I go to practice in these? I'm supposed to be on ice!"

"Absolutely, man! Let's get you out there. Excuse us, ladies," Elliot murmured as he walked past Ronni.

"Hey Mox," Ronni called out behind him. "Come see me in my office when you're done. Okay?"

With a wink her way, he closed the door behind him.

Chapter Five

Mission: Accomplished.

Elliot stood in the owner's box, looking down at the exhibition Mites game down below. Ryan stood in goal, his attention locked in on the action of the game in front of him, his moves quick and unbothered.

"Look at him, Mox," Bishop said, reaching around Moxley's shoulder with a slap. "He's a fucking natural!"

"I know. I just knew he'd kill it if he had the right gear on." Elliot paused, looking down at his phone. "Ronni is working on building a scholarship system through the Foundation. The feedback from Ryan and the staff is that it would be so much easier if funding wasn't a concern. I'm going to see if the guys want to chip in as well. Maybe hop in on practice days to say hi. It's great for the future of the game, you know?"

"Yeah, Mox, I know. Hopefully, we can help some more kids in the future."

"I hope so. Ronni just said I couldn't do the buying myself anymore," Elliot replied with a chuckle. "She has a solid point there, after all. I mean, you sent basically both our entire lockers into her office."

"That was unintentional. I didn't think everything would come in while we were on the road! How was I supposed to know that our equipment team was efficient?"

"Of course they are, dumbass; they're our equipment guys!" Bishop chuckled.

"Fine, you have a point," Elliot grumbled. "Still, she said I should have told her what I was up to first."

"She's not wrong. You didn't warn her you were using her office as a storage unit, and you didn't tell her until after she got pissed and stormed our locker room. Your communication skills suck, my man."

"Yeah, yeah, I know."

"Do I even want to know what you two are chirping about over there?" Bishop and Moxley turned to see Ronni entering the box, tablet in hand, and obviously still working on something. "Please tell me you're giving him a hard time about half-cocked ideas."

"Of course," Bishop replied. "Some day he's going to learn manners and not be a total shitshow."

Ronni smiled at the two men, their good-natured ribbing in counterpoint to the arena noise below.

"He still has some redeeming qualities, I guess," she said, as she sat her belongings in a chair.

Bishop looked at the couple. "I'm going to hop downstairs and surprise our goalie. You kids have fun." With a nod, he walked out of the suite, leaving Ronni and Elliot alone.

"He did that on purpose, didn't he?" Ronni asked, looking at Elliot.

"Yeah." He swiped at the hair that flopped in his face. "He said we needed to talk, Snow Queen. I need to apologize." She nodded in agreement. "I should have talked to you first, before moving forward with things."

"It would have made things easier," she agreed. "I could have set up everything while you were on the road. You just had to talk to me."

"I know. I just wanted to get it to him fast."

"So the next time you want to do sneaky charity things, you're going to..." she started, watching for him to finish the sentence.

"I'm going to tell you first so you can make it go seamlessly for me instead of surprising you with things."

"Good boy."

He shot a look her way and chuckled when he saw her grinning back at him.

Epilogue

Fifteen Years Later

"Callahan, get your ass over here!"

Ryan Callahan looked up at his name, seeing his coach with Gabby Moxley-Blackwood, daughter of Kane Blackwood, niece of hockey superstar Elliot Moxley, and the newest intern for the Rockville Ice Wolves. She had her blonde curls pulled up in a messy bun, tendrils falling into the hood of her logo sweatshirt, and she had a concerned frown on her face.

"What's up, Coach?" Ryan started as he crossed the locker room to the duo.

"We need you to do something for Moxley's charity," Gabby started.

"Easy, I'm on board. Whatever he needs, I'm there. No questions asked."

Coach raised an eyebrow. "Son, I know he's an idol of yours but maybe you want to hear what they need before you commit to something."

He shook his head. "Nope. Without Elliot Moxley, I wouldn't be here. When I say I owe that man my career, I mean I owe him my career."

Gabby smiled up at him. "It's really appreciated, Callahan, thanks for your help."

"Call me Ryan, please."

"Okay, so here's what I'm looking for," she started, pulling up a document on her tablet. "It has been 15 years since Elliot formed his gear program and we're trying to get sound bites from everyone who had received help. You were the very first recipient, and it would be awesome if I could get you to sit down for a short interview. What does your schedule look like?"

"You can have me whenever you want me outside of what Coach needs. I'm all yours."

"Great! I'll email you some dates and see what works best. Thank you, Ryan!"

"Anytime!" With that, Gabby walked out of the locker room, leaving Ryan standing next to Coach and his friends, who were waiting on him. "Damnit, I sounded like an idiot, didn't I?"

"Yeah, you did," a chorus of voices replied.

"You seriously need to chill out around her, you are so fucking obvious."

"I can't help it! She's so pretty and nice and I—"

"Will get your ass kicked by not one, but two former hockey players if you approach her," interrupted his best friend. "Maybe more than that. You know that her uncle's original line is basically family."

"I know. Why do you think I haven't asked her out yet?"

"Use me however you want. I'm all yours," he said in a fake voice. "Dude, you're so damn transparent with her."

"Shut up, Carson," Ryan grumbled, grabbing his gear to head out to the ice.

· · ·

***

Interviews were never Ryan's favorite part of being in sports, but he wasn't kidding when he said he would do anything for Gabriella Moxley-Blackwood. Maybe some day, when he wasn't just a no-name rookie on the Ice Wolves, maybe then he would be worthwhile of her time. Until then, he would just work hard, prove himself on the ice, and hopefully net the bigger contract soon.

It was because of this that he sat on a padded stool across from one of the top reporters in sports, as a makeup artist touched up the powder on his face. No pressure, he told himself, just don't throw up on the guy on live television in front of the love of his life. No big deal. Easy.

Why was it that playing in a packed arena was less nerve-wracking than this? Ryan inhaled a deep, calming breath before locking on his charming "face of the team" smile. Just behind the cameraman, he could see Gabby watching him carefully. His knee bounced nervously as he focused on the questions. He could feel the sweat run down his spine underneath his suit.

"Thank you so much for your time today," the reporter said, standing with his hand out.

"Anytime, thanks for having me," Ryan responded, taking his hand in a firm handshake. They posed for photos to go on social media, smiling broadly toward Gabby.

"Thank you for doing this," Gabby said to Ryan as the reporter and his team left the area.

"Anytime. This really means a lot to me." He shoved his hands in his pockets as he scuffed his toe against the tile. "I have a question for you, though."

"Sure, what's up?"

"Would you," he paused. "Would you ever consider having coffee with me? After work sometime?"

She smiled up at him, her cheeks glowing as she blushed.

"Yeah, I think I'd like that a lot, actually." Her smile grew bigger. "You know, that's how Uncle El started seeing Aunt Ronni, right?"

"Yeah, I heard something about that. I'm free now if you are."

"Sure, let's go!"

Sugar and Spice

Elliot Ason, Lori-Anne Cohen, Lacey Hall,
Jayne Katway, Eden Knox, Desi Leigh, Dawn Love,
Emily Michel, Kris Mitchell, K.R. Orinick,
Kate Prada, Lexy Ray, Katie Skye, E.C. Stakenas,
Erica Vance, Sheri L Williams, Liz Zerkel

Introduction

This was an entry in a charity anthology hosted by the Romance Riot. Proceeds were raised for RAINN between September 1-December 31, 2024. Each entry had a relating recipe, sticking to the "Sugar & Spice" theme, and then they were sorted in order of spice level: Green Pepper to Ghost Pepper. "Sugar and Spice and Everything Nice" was included in the section for "Habanero," due to the explicit language and nature of the intimate scene.

I wrote this after finishing "On the Power Play," which was a short for LoveSick Charity Anthology. Bridgette, Robicheaux, and Kozlov resonated with me, and I had already decided they would need a full novel at some point. It just felt natural to write them into Sugar & Spice as well. In Power Play, we meet Bridgette at a super low point; It's Valentine's Day, she's returning her engagement ring to her ex, and she sees him with a new girl already. Robicheaux enters the scene shortly after this, and has a moment to shoot his shot, and also show her ex that Bridgette is just as capable of moving on as he is. Of course Chad, her ex, takes offense to that, even though he had already moved on. Roby and Bridge then meet up with Kozlov. I can't wait to dig into the relationship between Roby and Koz, because they have such a beautiful back story that is just screaming to come out! So the three go out for dinner together, because the guys do this all the time, and they just naturally fold Bridgette into their plans.

In the various points of view, we see that the guys have had their eyes on her for some time, just waiting for the right time to make a move. Together. These two men are the best of friends, roommates, teammates, and are slowly closely linked to each other, it just feels natural for them to also share an intimate relationship with someone. So that is how we got the opening snapshot of our throuple, an impromptu Valentine's Day date that evolves into something more.

"Sugar and Spice and Everything Nice" picks up some time after "On the Power Play," where they trio are established in a relationship. The guys have been on the road for a string of games, and are due home soon. Bridgette does not live with the guys, but has access to their house.

Bridgette's point-of-view chapters highlight the growing conflict arc. She wants to recreate that initial meal for them, without going out. It doesn't go as planned, and in a moment of frustration, she orders in the food from the same restaurant. It isn't the home cooked surprise she wanted, and she's really stressed because of the state of the kitchen after her attempts had failed, and the mess in Kozlov's prized kitchen is overwhelming her.

Kozlov, being that black cat energy into the relationship, sees a mystery unfolding in between flights. What is Bridgette up to? He's not upset about her presence at the house, or the secret she seems to be keeping. He just wants to know why he has alerts of movement at the front door showing several different guys with bags coming by the house, and what she isn't talking about when he calls.

Robicheaux is always that golden retriever that is just happy to be there and all about the fun. He sees the mysterious alerters for what they are: She's surprising them with something. As the chapters move forward, and they get closer to home, Roby's excitement builds toward the climax of the story.

I can't get enough of these three, and I keep chipping away at the big novel of "On the Power Play." I can't wait for their love story (stories?) to come together for book 4 in the series!

So on that note, let's spend some time in The Sin Bin.

Love,

Eden

Chapter One

Kozlov

"Welcome aboard, thank you for flying with us," the flight attendant greets us as we board, but I barely looked up to see who was talking. I am hyper-focused, my eyes glued to my phone, the security camera footage from my front door playing on a loop. A man wearing, ironically, an Ice Wolves hat, backwards, approached the front door three times. Each time he held overstuffed, freakishly bright orange bags in his hands, and he walked back to his beat-up Camry empty-handed. What the actual fuck? Who is this guy, and what is he leaving at the door?

"Koz, you're gonna crack your phone again if you squeeze it any tighter." Roby's voice is soft beside me as he looks over my shoulder at the screen, watching the strange blue car back out of our driveway. "Who's that?"

"If I knew that, I would be less pissed about it. He dropped off a bunch of bags at the house, and I don't know why."

"Is Bridge there already?" I turn my head sharply, and

we both look at each other with narrowed eyes. "I'll text her to see if she's there."

"Wait...she disarmed the house early this morning." I scroll through the alarm log, watching the string of time-stamps next to her name over the past week. "What have you been up to, *Koshechka*?"

"What did the guy drop off?"

"Ugly orange bags." I scroll back to his last trip to the door and let the clip replay.

"Oh, I know those bags! That's how we used to order beer and groceries to the hockey house when we were too drunk or hung over to go get food!"

"Groceries? Why would she do that?"

"She eats too, you know. And if she wanted to stock the fridge for us before we got home? Dude, maybe you won't be cranky when we get up in the morning!"

I look over at Roby's face and scowl. He just grins wider, the stupid dimples in his cheeks, and then he giggles. Yeah, he giggles, just like Bridgette. Some days, having him around is like having an overgrown puppy. The barest bit of attention and he's lovesick. Why I put up with the sappy bullshit I'll never know, but he's grown on me.

"You're lucky I tolerate your ass most days," I grumble at him as I slide into the window seat, jamming my back-pack in front of me. Roby follows suit before dropping into the seat beside me, our forearms jockeying for position on the armrest between us. Whoever designed airplanes did not consider that occasionally, 6'5" giants would share rows. Normally, we try to get three-seat rows and keep the center empty between us; this was a smaller commercial line, so the best we could do was the two.

As the flight crew prepares the plane for takeoff, I start a text with the flight info to Bridgette. I'm sure she already knows, but she seemed to appreciate the consideration the last time.

We will be home around midnight, Koshechka.

Take your time.

This is not her usual response, I think, frowning. My head tilts, looking at the three words. Our girl never sends short texts; if anything, she's more likely to send a paragraph.

Is everything okay?

I watch as the three dots appear, then disappear repeatedly. This is more like her usual texting style, and I'll have a screen full of words in three, two....

Yep. Just fine.

Something feels very, very wrong here. With a grunt, I push the button to FaceTime her and watch as it rings. And rings.

Then the screen opens to show me the overhead light in my kitchen.

"Hi! Sorry, I'm, um," she pauses, and I hear metal clanging, a whispered curse. "Sorry, I had my hands full."

"What are you doing?"

"Nothing," she squeaks.

"Let me see your gorgeous face, Koshechka."

"Um..." she trails off. "I'm not pretty right now."

"You're always pretty to us. Now, what are you hiding?"

I hear her sigh, then rustle things around, before the screen angle changes to our girl. Her hair is in a messier bun than normal, her cheeks are flushed, and is that...chocolate on her cheek? Roby leans over his head, nearly on my shoulder as he looks at the screen as well.

"Whatcha doing, babe?" His statement is disarming, and I watch her bite her lip as she thinks about how to respond.

"I can't tell you yet. It's supposed to be a surprise."

"See, Koz, she's fine. We should leave her alone. We'll be home in a few hours, mon ami!" He waves at her before taking my phone and pushing the End button. "Seriously, you need to learn to relax a bit."

"What do you know, Roby?"

"Besides you needing to chill out a bit? We can trust her. She'll tell us when she's ready."

I side-eye him, unsure if I want to trust in his judgment.

Chapter Two

Bridgette

They say the way to a man's heart is through his stomach. I wonder if maybe there is a better way, because this is going to hurt doing twice the baking.

I sit in the middle of the giant kitchen, surrounded by mountains of canvas bags, and question every choice I've made in the last 24 hours. It seemed like a good idea at the time to bake for my boys—my boys!—as a "Welcome Home" present, since they have been on the road for the last nine days. I could have traveled with them but opted to stay back and keep up with the operations in the arena.

But they were coming home tonight, and now I wonder if I made an error in this plan. Duplicating their favorite desserts can't be that hard, after all. Triple chocolate torte and a cheesecake seemed simple enough when I pulled recipes off the internet and placed a pickup order for groceries to be delivered this morning. However, now that I have shortening and cocoa jammed under my fingernails, I am questioning all of my decisions.

It should not be this hard to make dinner for my boys.

But here I am, standing in the middle of a kitchen that looks like a tornado came through. Dirty dishes piled high in the sink, grease and flour on every surface, and worst of all... nothing edible.

After I realized that the cake and cheesecake would not work and I had incinerated the steaks, I placed a frantic order to Koz's favorite restaurant, Nico's. My heart shatters as my hopes for a perfect homecoming literally went up in smoke. And their poor kitchen will never recover from my presence. Why did I think I could do something like this?

I can't stop myself from pacing as I wait, hoping that at least the timing works out. If the apps are correct, the replacement food will get here just before the guys do. It will be close, but then at least the food will be warm. I head to the sink, hoping to start a load in the dishwasher and clean up the disaster I had made.

I contemplate leaving the mess and going upstairs to get the smell of burnt food off of me, but I can't just leave the kitchen like this.

It's fine, I tell myself, I'll just finish in here quickly and then go shower. I frantically fly around the kitchen, attempting to undo the mess that I made while keeping an eye on the clock. There wouldn't be enough time, panic making my heart flutter.

Chapter Three

Robicheaux

Flying with Kozlov is always a trip and a half. I know he's my best friend and all, but he really needs to learn to relax sometimes. Like right now. We're less than an hour from home, and he's wound so tight I'm surprised his head hasn't exploded yet. I can feel his knee bouncing where it rests against my own, even though from all outward appearances he's calm, earbuds in place, head leaning against the glass. To anyone who isn't me, he looks like he's asleep, but I know he's not.

"Psst, Koz," I whisper, leaning toward him. "You good?"

"What kind of question is that?" He cracks an eyelid, giving me a side-eye that would have anyone else running away, but I'm not fazed. I know underneath that cold, hard exterior he's a teddy bear.

"Koz, relax, man. She's fine." I drop a hand on his thigh, trying to stop the bouncing. Turning his head to face me, he stills, his eyes opening properly.

"Roby," he warns, dropping his gaze to my hand quickly before settling back on my face.

"Don't 'Roby' me, you're freaking the hell out. What's

wrong?" Giving his thigh a squeeze, I slide my hand back onto my leg. We're just two dudes flying together. No big deal.

"Our girl is alone at our house with some strange guy coming by. You're cool with that?"

"It's the grocery delivery guy. That's all."

"Who knows that she's there alone?" He bounces that leg again.

"Maybe. Maybe not. But we have that house secured like Ft. Knox. What's there to worry about?" Settling back on my seat cushion with a shrug, I wait for him to sort out his thoughts.

"I just don't like her being alone. Anything could happen."

"She's also independent, too. I think she can handle herself if need be."

"I wish she would have come with us this time." His grumbled answer is so soft, I barely hear it.

"I miss her too, man."

"Longest nine days ever." He sighs. "Next time, she comes with us."

"If she wants to."

"Yes, if she wants to." Adjusting his position with a grunt, he turns toward me. *That's better,* I think to myself. "It's weird knowing someone is waiting for us at home now."

"Weird good, or weird bad?" I'm sure I know the answer to this, but I want to hear him say it.

He chuckles, a smirk on his face. "Definitely good. For the longest time, we had no one at home."

"Thank God Turtle screwed up," I laugh, remembering how we got our start.

"It was bound to happen. I just wish she didn't get her heart broken first."

"I don't think that heartache lasted very long. And now she's ours."

"Damn right, she's ours," he echoes, his grin turning cocky.

Chapter Four

Kozlov

The fucking driver can't get us home fast enough. Roby has been trying to convince me that everything is fine, but my gut tells me there is something definitely wrong. Our girl is hiding something and I don't know what. The closer we get to home, the more I wonder—or maybe worry—what has happened while we were gone.

Approaching the neighborhood, I see a car pulling out of our driveway. It's not a car I recognize, so who was at our place? As we drive past, I look out the window at the driver. Again, a random guy. I trust Bridgette; I know I do, but who is she bringing to the house, while she is there alone? I grumble, my feelings all over the place. What the actual fuck?

We pull into the drive, and I open the door as soon as the driver puts the vehicle in park. I know I have bags in the back, but Roby can deal with them. I'm seeing Bridgette.

"Koz, the bags?" Roby calls out to me as I step up onto the front porch.

"Put them in the garage for now. I'll get them later."

It takes two tries for me to punch the numbers correctly into the keypad. *What the hell is wrong with you?* I grumble at myself as I finally get the code to work and throw the door wide.

My senses overload with everything. There is an acrid, smoky smell, and it looks like there is a haze in the air. Mixed with a fresh cleaning product scent I recognize, and then—I sniff again—air freshener, maybe? And then there is definitely steak in the mix.

I can hear Bridgette in the dining room, and I slowly step in that direction, following the sounds of packaging and —sniffling? I frown. Is she crying? As I ease closer to the door, I can hear her talking to herself.

"Such a dumb idea, Bridgette. Why did I think this would work? They're going to say they love it anyway, they have to. Oh, God, he's going to kill me for the kitchen, damnit, why was I so stupid?" I can hear the garage door hum into motion, and she squeaks in surprise. "Shit! No, no, no, no, I need more time!"

I peek around the door frame to watch her frantically rush to plate dinner from the takeout containers, muttering to herself. She is oblivious to me, so I ease slowly into the room, watching to see if she'll notice. Our sweet girl, working so hard. I smile, looking at the little fluffy apron she had put on over what looked like one of my t-shirts and black leggings, which appeared to have flour handprints on the thighs.

"What are you doing, Koshechka?"

Chapter Five

Bridgette

"What are you doing, Koshechka?"

The voice that would normally make me shiver and bite my lip instead made me jump, scream, and drop a dollop of mashed potatoes halfway on the lip of the plate and the rest onto the polished tabletop. My scream echoed as the spoon clattered out of my hands and onto the floor, leaving another potato print on the herringbone floor.

"Damnit!" I cursed, dropping into a defeated heap on the hardwood beside the spoon. The tears I had been holding back were no match for the adrenaline spike.

Yep. My reaction to seeing one of my boyfriends after two weeks? Bawling while sitting on the floor. Totally hot. I know.

"Shhh, no," Koz said softly, following me down onto the floor. "Why cry? It's okay." He folds me into his arms and just holds me tight.

"No, it's not!" I cried between sniffles. "I just wanted you to have a good home-cooked meal and-and I almost

139

burned down the kitchen, and-and," I paused. "I think I owe you new pans."

"I don't care about pans. I care about you." With that, he presses a kiss against my hair, whispering sweet Russian phrases as he rubs a hand down my arm.

"Babe, where are—oh, there you are," Roby says, coming through the back door, skidding to a halt in the doorway. "What's that smell?"

My tears launch all over again, as Koz pulls me into a tight hug, murmuring in my hair in Russian.

"I suck as a girlfriend," I mutter, looking at the potato splash on the floor.

"I will not have you saying those things or you will be punished. Da?"

I nod against his chest, taking comfort in his hold.

"Woah, is that the steak and lobster mashed potatoes from Nico? Oh, Babe, I love it!"

"J," Koz says over my head. "Nico's was not her Plan A for dinner."

I look up at Roby just as he does his head tilt, trying to work out what he's saying.

"What—" Roby starts.

"I tried to make it myself first," I mutter, my words muffled in Koz's chest. "I almost burned the kitchen down."

"That is the sweetest," Roby coos, coming over to us on the floor. "What happened to the potatoes?"

"I scared her," Kozlov admits. "It was an accident. Now, how about we finish up dinner? It has been a long trip, and I want to hear about what our sneaky kitten has been up to today." He stands to his full height, holding his hand out for me so I can have support. "We have missed you," he murmurs, pulling me into him so I can welcome him home.

My arms loop around his neck as I kiss him, feeling relief that I have him back again. "Roby was insufferable."

"I was no such thing. My turn," Roby counters, his hands sliding around me from the back and pulling me out of Koz's grip and into his own embrace. His large, warm hand shifts my chin so I can face him, kissing me softly in welcome as well. "God, I missed this."

"Roby, come, let her feed us before everything gets cold."

Chapter Six

Robicheaux

Our girl is the best fucking girl ever. I'm sure of it. No one else has a girlfriend like us and the most precious part? She doesn't even realize how amazing she is.

Sitting at the table with my two favorite people, locked in a debate over the latest news from the head office, I can't help but smile. This is what home feels like. I missed this. Sure, I ate dinner with Koz every freaking night, but he's not like this with just me. And that's fine, I get it. She brings out the best in both of us all the time. And now that we're, well, us, everything makes perfect sense. They make up the other part of me.

There is a lull in their conversation and they look at me, and I just know they're catching the dopiest grin on my face, but I can't care at the moment. Koz has a thoughtful look on his face as he pushes his plate away. Bridgette blushes as she looks between the two of us, and I wonder what else she had in her bag of tricks for the day.

"Koshechka, did you have dessert for us also?"

"I do," she says, moving to stand up and walk to the

kitchen. She returns with chocolate cake and cheesecake, exactly like we ordered on Valentine's Day. "I, um, I tried to make them but it didn't go the way I wanted to..." she trails off, her face falling as she sat everything down on the tabletop.

"It couldn't have been that bad," I say, as I move to pick up the cheesecake I favored.

"Yeah, it is that bad. I'm afraid I ruined the kitchen."

"There is no way you could have ruined the kitchen, Babe." I walk around, aiming to walk through the kitchen doorway myself to look.

"No, don't go in there!" she squeaks as she tries to stand in my path, blocking me. It was about as productive as a feather holding back a boulder, but she tried.

Koz took advantage of her distraction and made his way past us, and I heard him curse softly in Russian before looking back at us.

"What did you do?"

Chapter Seven

Bridgette

Busted.

Kozlov's face froze in shock at the destruction I left behind. I had to wonder what, exactly, he would do about the fact that left his professional-grade kitchen in shambles; the suspense had my heart lodged in my throat. He had designed it to precision, because cooking is definitely his thing, and I usually stay out of it. And the one time I thought I would try it, it went disastrously wrong.

"I'm sorry, Alexandr, I—"

"What happened?" Walking around the kitchen island slowly, he let his finger fall on a dusting of cocoa powder that I hadn't gotten up, leaving a clean line in the debris. The mixing bowls that still held some form of chocolate were touched next, and he licked the ganache off of his finger.

"I tried to make dinner." My voice cracked as I watched his slow inspection, and I could feel my chin quiver. The pan that held the charred remnants of the steak and herb butter was next on his tour, the spatula making a gritty noise as he poked it at the surface.

"What were you making us, kitten?" He made his way to the refrigerator where my printed recipes hung, hoping they would stay untarnished. "These are the exact things we order from Nico, yes?"

"Yes, sir." The whispered confirmation had him freezing to look at me. I knew what I said, and what it meant. The air hung heavy between us.

"Do you believe you need to be punished for this, Koshechka?"

"Maybe."

"You made a mess, didn't you?"

I whimpered. His tone hadn't changed, that deceptively soft voice not betraying his emotions. He could vibrate with anger about this and I couldn't tell. I kept my eyes trained on him as he continued his walk around the kitchen.

"Koz, what are..." Roby started, looking between the two of us. "Oh, I know what this means. Be gentle with our girl, okay? She tried her best."

"I don't think she wants it gentle, J." Kozlov walked up to me, close enough that all I could see was his travel suit and tie. He tucks a finger under my chin, lifting it so I had to look up and make eye contact with him. My breath quickened, and I bit my lip in anticipation. He cocks an eyebrow at me; it is his tell, even when he takes charge, he still asks for permission. Giving him a short nod, a slight increase of pressure against his fingertips for a split second.

It was all he needs to see before leaning in to kiss me.

Chapter Eight

Kozlov

Home is that feeling when I have Bridgette in my hands. It sounds so primal and might make me no better than a caveman, but this centers me. No matter what, kissing her calms me in a way that no meditation could ever touch.

I'm not even really mad about the kitchen. It's nothing that Marta can't fix in the morning when she's scheduled to be back in to clean. The pans that Bridgette thinks she ruined? No big deal. They were a gift from a sponsor, anyway.

My heart warmed, seeing all the hard work and effort she put into trying something new for us. She could have just ordered from Nico's and relaxed all day waiting on us, but she didn't. I'll have to have words with her about not telling me about it when I asked, but that's for later.

For now? I am home.

"That's our girl," I hear Roby say behind us as I slide my fingers into her hair, holding her in place so I can kiss her properly. Roby's hands slide between us, and I can sense him placing a kiss on the side of her neck. I feel drunk off of the combined smells of her, chocolate, and him. No wonder I catch her spraying his cologne on my things, or my cologne on his hoodie. The blend of us together? Intoxicating.

"Come here," I whisper against her lips, dropping my hands onto her hips. Breaking away from the kiss just enough I can see what I'm doing, I pick her up and set her on the island.

"Oh!" she exclaims as I set her on the edge. Before she can get another word in edge wise, I slot myself between her thighs, giving in to the desire to feel more.

"You were saying?" I say against her lips, reveling in the panting breaths against me. I can feel her fingers lightly against my shirt, a tentative touch feathering at my waistband. "Go for it, it's yours."

"Do we want to take this upstairs first?" Roby's glassy eyes look over at me for confirmation as he slides a hand inside of her oversized t-shirt.

"Not yet." Bridgette's nimble fingers slide my belt loose, and I grin. "I think our girl needs a lesson now."

Chapter Nine

Bridgette

Apparently, Alexandr Kozlov doesn't hold a grudge with destroying his prized kitchen.

Either that, or my punishment is pleasuring me to within an inch of my life. Funishment? Yes, please.

"Lay back, Koshechka." Roby's hands were soft, gently helping me down. Without thinking, my arms automatically crossed across my stomach. "None of that." My eyes fly open and I notice Kozlov pulling off his tie. "Tie her hands down, Roby," he orders, tossing his tie at him. Roby doesn't miss a beat, snatching the silk and standing over my head. Right behind me, I knew there was a towel rack. With careful hands, Roby slides my hands over my head and ties me down to the rack. I'm fully exposed with my arms stretched over my head, my shirt raising with the motion.

"Let's get this out of the way too," Roby says as he slides my shirt up even higher and onto my restrained wrists. "Beautiful," he breathes, soft fingers tracing the straps on my bra.

"You naughty girl, hiding pretty things from us," Kozlov

says, sliding my leggings past my hips to see the matching panties. "You did that on purpose, didn't you?"

"Maybe." I bite my bottom lip, waiting for him to say something about my cheeky retort. He growls, sliding his hands up my bare calves.

"You know how I feel about these, don't you?"

"Yes, sir."

"And how I feel about you hiding your pretty things?"

"Yes, sir."

"What happens when you try to hide your pretty things from me?"

"I-I get," I pause, words stolen from me as he places a kiss on the inside of my knee. "I get corrected."

He hums in agreement, sliding his lips up my thigh as Robicheaux lowers the cups on my bra. I squeak as they move in tandem, Koz pressing a hot open-mouthed kiss against my center as Roby takes a nipple between his teeth.

My vision dims as my eyes roll back in my head. I am in so much trouble.

Chapter Ten

Robicheaux

Bridgette laid out like our personal buffet is probably my new favorite use of the island.

Watching her back arch and freeze is like looking at a fine piece of art. She doesn't know how gorgeous she looks right now; her pale skin glistening. I know she's super self-conscious about being exposed sometimes, but with us around? We try to show her every way we can that she's perfect. Alexandr is relentless, devouring her, and the whole time his eyes locked on her.

Even I have to admit, it's hot to watch.

I stand and walk toward her head, making eye contact with Koz as I lower my mouth to hers.

"Look at him, Bridge. How does it feel? He's been dreaming about doing this all damn week. You want to know how I know?"

"How?" she pants, gasping as he does something wicked with his fingers.

"I heard about it all week long." Kissing her neck, I slide my hands around her bound arms to cup her breasts again. "God, I've missed you. This. Us."

"Tell me more," she gasps, "please." Koz growls against her, nipping the soft curve of her thigh. I shoot him a look; I'm going to pay for this later.

"Remember when we talked on video in Orlando? I heard him rub one off in the shower afterward." I pause for effect, her whimper breaking the silence. Leaning back down by her ear, I whispered, "Twice."

"And," she sighs. "What about you?"

"What about me, kitten?"

"Did you…" Her words trail off as she moans again.

"If you can talk, we're doing it wrong," Koz says from between her thighs. "Roby, how about you find something else to do with that smart mouth of hers?"

"Yes, please," she whispers, straining against the tie to brush her fingers against my pants.

I unfasten my belt, lowering my zipper slowly while she cranes her head back to watch the show. I take my time teasing her, biting my lip when she bites hers as she stares at me hungrily.

"You want something?"

"Yes," she whispers, licking her bottom lip.

"Use your words, kitten."

"Please, Roby," she begs, reaching out for me.

"Please what?" I slip out the top of my boxer briefs, giving myself a healthy squeeze as I ease closer, but still out of her reach. "Is this what you want?" I ask as I run my mushroomed head across her bottom lip.

Fuck, she's gorgeous like this.

I can't tease her anymore.

Sliding myself into her warm mouth, my eyes roll back as I take in all the sensations. Even with her hands tied down and at our mercy, she has complete control of the situation. I can't imagine anywhere else I'd want to be, except maybe to trade places with Koz.

I make eye contact with him for a split second before his clouded gaze focuses hard on Bridgette's mouth, which is busy swallowing me whole. With a nod from me, he shoots to his feet, fighting to get his own belt off and standing between her soft thighs.

"God, Bridge, if you could see yourself now, so damn hot," I murmur at her, feeling her hum around my length. "Koz is so ready for you. Are you ready for him, love? We've been waiting for weeks to have you all spread out like this, at our mercy. You like it when we're like this, don't you?" Her hummed assent intensifies as she moans loudly around me, and I look over just in time to watch Koz slam balls deep into her.

Fuck, I think to myself. I rock my hips a little more, giving Bridge some more length. Watching her like this drives me so, so close to the edge.

Koz is spewing absolute filth in Russian as he grinds deeper into her. Nope, I stand corrected. This. This is the sexiest thing ever, and I'm not even ashamed to say it.

A groan leaves her and she arches. The combined attack of both my words and Koz's touches drives her closer to the edge until she finally shatters.

Beautiful chaos.

Her cries echo off the walls, and we don't let up, keeping her in that freefall.

Chapter Eleven

Kozlov

There are few things I enjoy more than watching our prim and proper love come unraveled.

Bridgette practically screams around Roby's dick as she clenches down on my own. I grit my teeth and breathe deep, trying not to follow her into that free fall.

Not yet.

Roby pulls away from her mouth, breathing deeply as he tries to get himself back under control. *The feeling is mutual;* I think to myself. I hold absolutely still, reveling in the feeling of the small flutters around me.

Bridgette pants, each exhale an expletive as she calms down.

Epic. Little Miss "I don't curse" releases a drawn out "fuck" and I step out of the way, motioning for Roby to come in my direction. He steps between her thighs, easing into her slowly. As he sets their own rhythm, I smooth my hand along her satiny skin. I missed her softness to our hard edges on our last trip. It isn't the same without her between us on the long trips.

My fingertips dance across her tight nipples and she

arches into my touch, the motion rolling her into a slow grind against Roby, who grunts in response.

"Beautiful girl, look at how well you take him," I say, allowing my fingers to trace her collarbone, lay my palm against her pulse in her neck, and hold her jaw. "This was the longest week ever. Knowing you were all the way over here and I couldn't touch you," I leaned down, sealing our lips together, "it was torture."

"But you had Roby to keep you company."

"I did," I agree, moving to kiss the spot below her ear that she loves. "But he doesn't smell like you." Standing, I move behind her, where Roby had been. "Or feels like you," I said, smoothing my hands behind her head to massage her neck a bit, before sliding my hands down her arms to my tie. "He also won't let me tie him to the island like you."

Her gasp turns into a giggle, and I know Roby surprised her with an aggressive thrust. "Oh, you poor, neglected thing." Her newly freed hands found my hardened dick, making me hiss with pleasure. "May I please?"

Stepping forward, I watch intently as she wraps her lips around my head before pulling me forward by the hand at the base of my shaft.

"Look at you, you always take us so well, Koshechka." I press my hips forward more, sliding more of my length into her waiting mouth. "That's our girl, so beautiful."

"So fucking hot watching you two," Roby pants, his thrusts falling a little uneven. He's close, I can tell. I'm not too far behind him.

"Throw her legs up on your shoulders. Get in there deep," I order him. His eyes flutter closed, and I just know that the impact of my words is going to tip him off the edge. He does as he's told, grasping her shin and placing a soft kiss on the side of her ankle. Bridgette makes another one of those greedy moans, and the vibration shoots sparks up my spine. Yeah, we're not going to last long with her tonight.

"Shit, Koz, I'm about to—" Roby groans, Bridgette gasps, and I'm tumbling into the abyss with both of them. The chain reaction gets me every goddamn time.

Chapter Twelve

I missed this so much.

Cuddled between my two men in our bed, Roby nestling behind me with my head pillowed on Koz's chest, I feel like all the stress from the road trip has faded. My fingernail traces the Cyrillic letters on his opposite pectoral, and I smile to myself.

"You're still awake," Kozy murmurs, picking up my restless hand so he can place a kiss on my palm.

"For the moment, yeah," I whisper back, being careful not to wake up Roby. His slow, even breaths fluff my hair.

"And why? Do you need something?"

"No, I'm just," I sigh. "Content."

"Just content?"

I laugh. He would take contentment as a substandard response. That's not surprising.

"I'm just happy you're both back, and you aren't mad about the kitchen."

"Koshechka, why would I be mad about the kitchen? You wanted to make something meaningful. It wasn't your fault that you were trying to make new things and it didn't work out."

"But the pans, and the mess— "He cuts me off.

"—Will be taken care of later. Marta will be in to clean around nine. Now rest, my love, before you wake up Roby. He says I'm cranky when I wake up too early? You should see him."

I chuckle, trying to imagine my golden retriever boyfriend being the grumpy one.

"You know, chocolate chip pancakes will fix that right up, right?"

Kozlov freezes. "You're serious? Pancakes will get him out of that tantrum?"

"Every single time," I promise. "I do it every early morning skate for him."

"Bastard," he grouses, looking over at Roby's floppy curls behind me.

"I'll have you know my parents were married two years before they had my sister, and for a full five years before they had me. I'm definitely not a bastard."

"Do you want chocolate chip pancakes for breakfast, too?"

"No, Koshechka, I just want you for breakfast." he kisses my head again, the only part he can reach, and I run my hand up and down his side in a soothing pattern.

"I think that can be arranged."

Vengeance
for
Valentine's

Introduction

Introducing new characters into the series without plans of a full novel feels strange. When the offer for "Vengeance for Valentine's" went out in the Hype Girls Discord, I couldn't see using any of the current cast for it. The theme for V4V? Revenge is a dish best served hot. Karmic retribution, just in time for a holiday built around love and hearts. Vengeance raised money for the American Heart Association between February and May 2025. Every short in the book tied back to our original series bases, and each offered up a great twist on karma, with our characters getting their just rewards, and the antagonists getting a serving of humble pie.

To a degree, I was influenced by "Jesse's Girl." Yes, that song from the 80's about a guy pining away for his best friend's girl. I could see that playing out in the Ice Wolves universe; a former player, maybe still close by and seeing one of his former teammates dating his crush but treating her badly, and then he finally gets his shot. The hard part is figuring out if he can get over his own shortcomings, because he isn't a player anymore. Also, what did it say that he wanted this girl and she just thought of him as a good friend?

When she comes back to the bar because it is – and by connection, Ronan is – a safe space, he starts to crack. And when she asks why she wasn't enough? All bets are off. I loved writing how Ronan was twisted up about doing the "right thing," and giving them a quick interlude that felt like the close of a slow burn.

Will they never get a full novel? I'll never say never. Ronan has cameos in "Tripping" and pops up throughout the series. Emory may make a cameo or two as well, after this. Building the Ice Wolves family, one relationship at a time.

Let's spend some time with "RoJo" and Emory.

Love, Eden

Chapter One

Ronan

Of all the bars in a city this big, she had to keep walking into mine. I would know that face anywhere.

Warm chocolate brown eyes I could get lost in? Check.

Bright smile that never fades? Double check.

Legs for days? Yeah, big check.

Wearing the jersey of the biggest dick on the Rockville Ice Wolves? Unfortunately, yes, she was.

Emory was way too good for Kyle Windsor, but then again, she was also way too good for a washed-up, has-been pro player with a bum knee working behind a bar. Still, she's the girl I couldn't stop thinking about. I could only hope that someday she would dump the ass before he could really hurt her, and then maybe she could be the WAG, wife or girlfirend, that I could have. Or wanted. WAGs don't look at former players like me.

My eyes found her, like they always did, and I watched her slide onto the barstool, her tall black boots bareley reaching the railing. I gave myself three solid heartbeats to sink into that warm feeling before locking it down. She wasn't mine, and I had to respect that. Even if I didn't respect that man.

"You're over here early," I commented, setting a black napkin down under her drink. I didn't even have to ask her for her order. I knew it by heart. Vodka cranberry, no ice, two lime twists.

"I wanted to catch Kyle before he headed in for warmups, but I guess I missed him." Her left hand twisted the stir stick in random shapes through the pink drink, twirling around the lime slices.

I could feel in my gut that if he said he was coming in for warmups, he's still ridiculously early. They're never this early, or they never were when I played. My gut churned, hoping he wasn't playing the "working early/late" card to see someone else on the side.

"You can hang around here until the doors open," I offered. "Help yourself. You know where everything is, right?"

She nodded, smiling warmly at me. My gut churned, knowing that I could save her from him. I just have to say the words. But I couldn't do that to her. She deserved more than just a has-been pro working late nights behind his own bar, even if it is the most popular hockey-themed bar in the arena district. The Sin Bin, the slang for 'penalty box,' the place I was infamous for, is now my career and livelihood. All my free time and money goes into this; there's no time for conventional dating outside of this.

Instead, I just let her be. I'll give her a shoulder to cry on, a fresh drink, and make sure she gets to her car safely every night.

Chapter Two

Ronan

Every week, she came in. And every week, her shine dimmed just a little.

I shouldn't have been watching her as closely as I do. She wasn't mine. She belonged to a friend of mine. Maybe "friend" is too strong of a word. A teammate, coworker at best. If anything, I don't really like him. He had a shit attitude and wasn't a team player, so I certainly didn't miss playing with his selfish ass.

Why she chose him is beyond me. I saw how he treated her like an afterthought. She did everything she could for him, fully committed, and he couldn't even act like they were together in public. She was impossibly bright and had given up so much time for him, and all for what? If she was mine, there would be no doubt about it. She would receive that acknowledgement. She wouldn't have to sneak around and hide her relationship status. I shouldn't wish ill on anyone, but I couldn't wait for her to dump his ass. I was sure she would, eventually. She seemed so tired.

Even as I watched her typing away on her lwaptop, finishing up the last of her work before the game tonight, my heart lurched for her. She looked exhausted and still had hours to go before she might rest. Without a second thought, I poured her a coffee, setting it next to her with the cream and sugar.

"I didn't— oh, hey, Ronan."

God, I loved it when she called me that. The boys, they all called me Joey, Joe, RoJo, or RJ, occasionally, but she was still the only one who called me Ronan. A lifetime as a hockey player gave me dozens of nicknames. To hear my full name from her just felt different. Special.

"You look like you can use this," I said, nudging the mug closer to her.

"Thanks. You're always taking such good care of me." Her smile wavered a little.

"Are you okay?" The question popped out of my mouth before I could even consider telling my brain to shut up and stay professional.

She sucked her bottom lip in between her teeth, brow furrowed as she thought over the question. Shoulders lifting slightly, she sighed, picking up two sugar packets.

"Kyle is," she paused, her fingers twisting the edge of the paper packets restlessly. "He's stressed, I think. It's hard to be around sometimes."

"He's not hurting you, Em, right?"

Her surprised face gave me some reassurance he's not, or at least not enough that she's picked up on.

"No, nothing like that. He's just under a lot of pressure by the team and I haven't been able to support him as much."

"What do you mean? You're here for every home game and you've been by for practices. Are you still running his social media for him, too?"

"Yeah, apparently he thinks his follower numbers are low, and his jersey isn't the top selling, so he's frustrated."

"And he says that's your fault? Seriously?"

"He's just...frustrated."

"So I heard," I murmured. "He's really not hurting you, right?"

"No," she responds, her chin shifting sideways jerkily. "He's just loud about it."

"Words can hurt too, Em."

"He doesn't mean it. He'll be fine at the All-Star break, he just needs to make it there."

I nodded my head, even though I didn't totally agree. All-Stars were just more stress than regular season, especially if he was chosen for the conference team. If he wasn't, I worried about the backlash she'd experience since it sounded like he was having problems coping with the workload.

Between us, her phone danced on the counter; the screen flashing a photo of Kyle. She picked up her phone, tucking it between her ear and her shoulder as she listens to the call. My heart jumped as she straightened, her face pale.

"Ky, I — No, I know, I told them — I can only push your social media so far!" Her bottom lip went white beneath her teeth. If she kept biting down like that, she'd draw blood. "I'll try to fix it, I promise. I know. I won't go anywhere tonight until I hear. Okay, I lo—" Her shaky hand pulled away from her head, the screen back to that familiar home screen of Kyle.

She tried to say "I love you" and he hung up on her. Idiot.

"You good, Em?" I leaned across the bar, keeping my words as soft as I could with the jukebox playing in the corner.

"It's fine," she muttered, cracking her neck before typing furiously again.

"That didn't sound fine."

Her teeth dug into her bottom lip, turning the tender flesh pink. Anger flashed in her eyes as she focused on her screen, and she was right back where she had been before he called.

"He's stressed. He's just lashing out because of it."

"Em," I sighed. "Never in the time of ever did I yell at my personal assistant, and that included after shattering my knee in the Cup finals. You shouldn't have to hear this from him."

"Just have to make it to the off-season," she muttered, not looking up.

Chapter Three

Emory

I hadn't even pulled into my driveway yet and my eyelid was already twitching. My headlights traced across the front of my house. No, not mine, his.

A shiver trickled down my spine, and I groaned against the nausea that hit as my stomach flipped. Coming back here got harder and harder each time. I didn't know why I was still with him, or why I still lived there. Home should be a place of solace, peaceful, and a refuge. But mine was a warzone.

The living room lights reflected cheerily off the snow outside, adding warmth to the frigid exterior. What usually looked welcoming is instead ramping up my anxiety, because that probably meant he made it home already. Shit. I hoped I had some time before I had to see him, especially if he had seen the email about getting cut from the latest round of commercials for upcoming games.

"Put your big girl panties on already," I grumbled, gathering my purse and keys. Wind whipped around me, tossing my hair in my face. Winters here positively blow.

Throwing the door wide, I listened carefully for where he might be. I relaxed as I heard the surrounding silence, but froze when I heard him.

"Oh shit," he cursed from upstairs.

I repeated the phrase in my head also, thinking he heard me come in, except for what I heard afterward had me wondering if our phrases meant different things.

"Don't stop. Please, don't stop. Just like that."

What—or who—is he saying that to?

My steps landed softly on the carpeted stairs, watching for the creaking board halfway up. There's no way this is live. He recorded us and is playing it back, right? It has to be. There's no way he had a woman—

"Oh, Kyle, yes, right there!"

I froze. He had a woman in our—his—house and in our —*his*—bed. My knees buckled under me, sending me tumbling to the floor at the top of the stairs, spilling the contents of my purse across the landing in front of me.

"Shit, no no no," I muttered, scrambling to catch everything.

Time seems to freeze and all I can hear is my heart beat pounding in my ears.

"What was that?" The feminine voice hissed, and I just know I'm going to get caught—

Wait. A. Minute. Who cares if I'm out here? I live here!

I stuffed everything back into my bag and stood, trying to look nonchalant as I heard rustling coming from behind our—his—bedroom door.

I looked at my watch, wondering how long it's going to take, or should I do some wild soap opera shit and burst into the room on them.

Before I could move, the bedroom door cracked open and I could see Kyle peeking through at me.

"What the fuck, Emory? I thought you weren't coming home tonight!"

"Obviously. Who's your friend?" I nodded at the shocked blonde peeking from behind him. "I've seen you hanging around the locker room before, right?"

"Yeah, I—" she started, but he cut her off with a whisper.

"Don't worry about her," he grumbled. "You know I've been stressed the hell out about the roster. And you're never home! What the hell was I supposed to do, Em?"

I nodded, thinking of all the other things he had said and done while "stressed."

"Cool. Guess I'll leave you to...destress."

I turned to go back down the stairs, the picture of indifference. I wouldn't dare be caught crying, and I'd be damned if I went into hysterics in front of them. To hell with all of that. I'm fine, I'm cool, I'm... falling. Arms pinwheeling, I froze in suspended animation for a split second before gravity slammed me down against the stairs.

Hard.

Breath whooshes out of my lungs and agony shoots through me as I feel the edges of the carpeted stairs slamming into my body.

"Fuck! Emory, are you okay?" Kyle's panicked voice called down to me, muffled by the wooshing in my ears. "Em! Jesus, say something!"

I took a shallow breath, testing out my tender lungs, and groaned as I tried to get up.

"Don't worry about it," I gritted out between clenched teeth. Why the hell can the ground never actually swallow you up when you're mortified?

Ignoring the chatter at the top of the stairs, I gathered my nearby belongings and walked out the door for the last time without even a backwards glance. I didn't need to hear his bullshit; I was finally fucking free.

Chapter Four

Emory

God, I hated crying. I swear, if I cried one more time, I was going to scream. My throat hurt from the sobs, my eyes felt dry and gritty. My face ached like a son of a bitch and I must have cut myself because it burned like hellfire when my tears hit it. And all for what? He's just a guy; I should hit him with my car.

But he was more than that. I thought he loved me. I broke my lease for him. I gave up my job for him, just so I could be at his beck and call as his "assistant."

Only for him to bring home some girl from a party when he thought I wouldn't be around.

As if it wasn't enough of a shock to find him in bed with someone else, I made an ass of myself by falling down the stairs like I'm in a damned telenovela. In my own home!

No, not my home. He never put me on the lease. Technically? I didn't know where I was going to go tonight. I just knew I wouldn't come back there.

Which is why I approached the one place in this city where I knew I'd be safe with the one person I knew I could depend on.

The Sin Bin. Ronan will listen to my sob story, pour me a drink, and maybe he'll know some place safe for me to go until I can get my feet under me again.

Shoving open the door, I was assailed by the sound of karaoke night in full blast. Well, at least I wouldn't be alone. I hopped up onto my usual stool gingerly and laid my throbbing head down on the glossy surface, relishing in the cool wood against my burning cheek.

"Emory?" The noise of off-key karaoke almost drowned out my name. I lifted my head wearily, anyway, trying to smile at Ronan only to cringe as my cheek throbbed again. His warm smile darkened the closer he got. "Jesus Christ, who did this to you?" A warm, rough hand grabbed my chin, vibrating with anger, tilted my head this way and that. "I'm going to fucking kill them."

"Is it really that bad?" I asked softly. I glanced at it in the mirror and thought it could've been worse, but it had its own pulse.

"Come with me. Let's get you put back together."

His tone left no room for arguement, so I followed him in resignation to his office, trying to walk normally. He pulled the door closed behind us. The abrupt muting of the off-key singing was a relief.

"It's not—"

"It's not what it looks like? Really, you're going to say that? I mean it, Em, who the hell hurt you? It looks like you lost a fight with a cat."

"Puck bunny," I corrected, wearily.

"Excuse me?"

"It was a puck bunny. He took one home, and I walked in, and — well, I don't think I can go back. I know I can't go back." I swallowed hard against a knot in my throat. "I don't have anywhere else to go, my stuff is all there, and I—"

"Stay here. Give me a couple hours to hand off to a manager for the night and you can stay at my place until you get a better idea. Cool?" I nodded, walking to the couch. The cushions swallowed me as I sat, and I watched him gather a first aid kit from a cabinet. "Let's get that cleaned up first. She really did a number on you."

I couldn't even correct him. She never touched me. "It'll be fine. I'm just worried about my stuff, really. I left almost everything behind." My gut dropped. "I think I left my laptop behind, even. How the hell am I going to work now?"

"Em, pause. You should take some time to recover and get your bearings straight first. Let me get you put together first."

With gentle hands, he cleaned up the scratch, inspecting the rest of me for damage, handling me like I was something delicate and fragile. I should hate this. I'm not delicate or fragile.

"I gave up everything for him and this is how he treats me. That's the part that irritates me the most. All of my sacrifices so he could do that. Like, did he even care about me?"

He grumbled something that sounded a lot like, "coulda told you that," before shaking his head.

"He didn't deserve you," he said out loud instead.

"But you could've told me that?" His soft touches paused, and he looked up at me with wide eyes.

"I." Clearing his throat softly, he took a deep breath before restarting. "It seems rude to tell you that now."

"It's true though," I countered.

Bowing his head over our now joined hands — when did that happen — he nodded.

"He didn't deserve you or the effort. You worked yourself tirelessly to keep his social media visible, keep him happy. And he didn't appreciate you."

"I know you're right, it just—" A sob cut off my words, making my throat tight. Burning tears slipped off my eyelashes and there's nothing I can do to hold any of it back. "God, I'm so sick of crying about it. About him."

Strong arms wrapped around me, and I allowed myself to sink into his warmth and comfort. Shushing noises whispered past my ear on a breath, and for the first time in forever, I actually felt a calm settle over me.

Chapter Five

Ronan

Grinding my teeth, I walked down the stairs, my boots thudding in cadence with the ache in my chest and my heart pounding furiously against my ribcage. Jesus, what the hell was he thinking? And letting her get hurt like this?

I wanted to hunt him down and bloody up his stupid, pretty face in retaliation for her.

I wanted to beat him to a pulp for breaking her heart.

I couldn't do any of these things right now because she's in my bar, in my office, waiting for me.

Flagging down my staff felt like it took ages, but finally they had their responsibilities and I could go back to her. With a fresh bottle of water and a bar towel full of ice, I walked back into my private office. She looked so small curled up on my couch, pulling my jacket tight around her. It wasn't super cold in there, but I wouldn't be surprised if she's in shock after the adrenaline crash.

"Emory? Are you okay?"

"Yeah, I'll be fine. I just have a lot of things to figure out, and fast."

I couldn't have her feeling helpless like this. Sliding onto the couch beside her, I took her frigid hands in mine. Her skin was so soft, I wonder what they would feel like against me.

Stop objectifying the woman minutes after she leaves a broken relationship, you horny asshole!

"How can I help?"

"I just need to call an Uber and get to a hotel for the night. I can figure it out in the morning, after I have time to relax."

"Stay with me." The words popped out of my mouth before I could even think it through. "I have plenty of space, and I'm never there. You can have free rein of it until you get things figured out."

"Ronan, I couldn't—"

"Please. I insist. You'll have a safe place and you won't have the expenses of a hotel room. Stay as long as you need."

Sighing in resignation, she nodded. She had to know I was right, after all. Hotels would get expensive fast, and it's not like I was a total stranger.

"Okay, you're right. I'll just stay here until you're ready to go."

"Make yourself comfortable, Em, and come get me if you need anything." My hands picked up hers again, my thumbs running across her reddened knuckles. "It's going to be okay, I mean it."

Chapter Six

Emory

I woke up to the comforting smell of leather and wood smoke.

Wait...wood smoke? I didn't remember being around a fire. Where am I? Prying my gritty eyes open, I tried to take in my surroundings. I was on a couch in an office? A messy desk sat across from me, the room lights dimmed, and I had an Ice Wolves blanket wrapped around me. I could see lights flashing through a window, and a glance through showed me the interior of the Sin Bin, Ronan's bar. The last stragglers seemed to be headed toward the door, and I could see Ronan and the rest of his team cleaning up around the bar and tables. It was a strange feeling, looking down on a place I had been so familiar with. Almost as if he could feel my gaze on him, Ronan's eyes shot toward the window, searching for me. My breath whooshed out of my lungs with a gasp. Kyle definitely never made me feel like that just by looking in my general direction. What the hell? Am I really feeling things for someone else already?

I watched him turn back to the bartender busily wiping

down the bartop, and hitch his thumb toward the door. After the bartender nods, Ronan headed toward the stairs we took earlier. Squeaking, I threw myself on the couch, trying to look nonchalant and like I wasn't just ogling him. The doorknob turned slowly; the door creaking softly on the hinges. An accoustic cover of a pop hit was humming softly behind him before he shut the door.

"You're awake." He smiled softly, eating the space between us in long strides, coming across to sit beside where I was on the couch. "Are you okay with driving? You can follow me, or we can take your car. I don't mind leaving mine here."

"I'm ready. I just don't feel up to driving."

"I'll drive yours. Whenever you want to leave, you can go, and I can hitch a ride back. I don't want you to feel trapped."

"I don't think you could ever make a girl feel trapped, Ronan," I said, pushing wearily to my feet.

Chapter Seven

Ronan

She hadn't let go of my hand getting up off the couch, and she only let go of me when I tucked her into the passenger seat of her car and walk to the driver's side. As soon as I settled in and placed my hand on the shifter, she latched on again like I'm a lifeline.

I wouldn't dream of telling her to let go, and I shouldn't even want to get into how goddamn perfect our hands feel together or how my lizard brain has been entertaining the theory that other parts may fit together, either.

Her gaze locked on the front of my house as the headlights came across the front porch. My heart pounded. What the hell was I thinking dragging her here? Does she even really want to be here? Did she just say it to be nice? What kind of asshole drags a woman who just left a broken relationship home away from a public setting to his house in the goddamn woods?

"You good, Emory?"

She startled in the seat beside me, wide eyes turning toward me from the view of my house. She huffed out a muffled, "Yeah, fine," before reaching a shaky hand out for the door handle.

"Wait, I'll get that for you." I ran around the hood of her car as fast as my bum leg would take me. I grab the handle just as she pushes open from the inside.

"Thanks," she whispered before taking my offered hand and letting me keep it in mine as we went into the darkness.

"Let me show you to the guest room, and then I can bring you some fresh towels. Did you have anything in your car, or—"

"I don't even have anything to sleep in. Or wear tomorrow. Everything is at his place." Her steps faltered, the realization hitting her. "Jesus, I literally have nothing on me but my purse. I have to go back there."

I shook my head. "Don't worry about that right now. I have some things that will get you by for now. We can figure it out in the morning, okay?"

"I hate the idea of waiting. And it gives him time to do something stupid like thrash my things."

I froze, staring down at her. "Do you think he will? Honest question. I'll go over there right fucking now if you think he will." My voice, gritted through clenched teeth, is almost unrecognizeable.

She shrugged helplessly. "I don't know, honestly. I thought I knew him, that he wouldn't be the kind to do that, but I also didn't think he was the guy to cheat on me, either. God only knows how long that was going on."

"We can go over first thing in the morning. He still doing the early morning practice?"

"Yeah. He should be out of the house by 6:00."

Wrapping a hand carefully around her back, I led her toward the stairs.

"Cool, so let's get some sleep so we can fix this all in the morning. Pretty sure Ma left girly smelling things in there so you can take a shower. I'll bring you fresh towels and something to sleep in."

I watched her walk around the room, setting her purse down on the dresser before sitting on the edge of the bed heavily. Before I let myself something stupid, I head across the hall to my room, grab one of my t-shirts and gym shorts, and come back to her.

She had gotten up and stood in front of the bathroom mirror, staring hard at her own reflection. The bathroom light washed her out, accenting the puffy bags under her eyes, and a tear trailed over the angry skin.

"Em, sweetheart," I called softly to her, setting the pile on the counter by her hand.

"Ronan, can I ask you a question?"

"Anything,"

"Why wasn't I enough for him?"

Chapter Eight

Emory

"What kind of question is that?" He shook his head, his gaze locked on mine. "Emory, babe. You are not the problem. He is."

"No, I have to be the problem. Why did he feel like taking another woman to bed was the right answer? What's wrong with me?"

He clenched his jaw, lips pressed tight like it could keep the words in. Words I desperately needed to hear from someone because the voice in my head, the one thast usually told me all the negative things about myself, was getting too loud for me.

"Em, I mean this in the nicest way possible. If there was anything wrong, it was you were too much, too good for him. He had no idea what he had in front of him." He stepped closer, standing just behind me, taking my right hand in his own. "You deserve to be treasured, and I don't think he was up to taking care of you. The issue is all about him. You're perfect."

A humorless chuckle left me. "I bet you say that to all the girls."

His head shifted sideways, his eyes drifting shut. Looking down, his left hand started snaking around my stomach, his broad hand making me feel so small in his embrace.

"No. Just you."

I gasped, his eyes laser focused on my own.

"You mean—"

"Emory, I don't make a habit of begging or bullshitting. I meant what I said."

"What—how should—what would you have done?"

"What would I have done if you were my girl?"

I left his question hanging in the tense air between us, half-afraid to talk past the knot in my throat again. I settled for nodding my answer instead.

"Say it. Out loud."

"Tell me, Ronan. Please."

His sigh ruffled the small hairs against my neck, and he closed in, pressing my back flush against him. Laying my head back against his chest felt like the most natural thing in the world. I felt the next words out of his mouth vibrated through me.

"For starters, I would never look at another woman like I do you. You would never wait for anything, and especially not by yourself in a bar."

I couldn't help the soft smile on my face. "But what if I'm waiting for you, and I'm in your bar?"

He grunts in disapproval. "Don't be a brat, Em." He takes a deep breath, his nose pressing into my hair just behind my ear. "I would worship the ground you walked on if you'd let me, hoping I would be worthy enough to even get a smile from you."

"Oh, Ronan," I whisper, his sincerity making my heart swell.

"You have no idea how much it hurt watching him take advantage of you, over and over again. To know if I had just a moment with you, I could show you what you're worth."

"It should've—" The words blurt out of my mouth before I can stop them.

"It should've what?"

"It should've been you. From the beginning." I turned within his arms, pressing back against the counter.

"Em, don't play with me like that. I'm serious."

"So am I," I return, refusing to budge an inch.

"You're hurting right now, lashing out because he—"

"I said what I said Ronan. You've treated me more like a girlfriend than he has for months, and you haven't even touched me." His heart pounded furiously behind his ribcage, in sync with my own. "Please, I just need to feel something. Make me forget."

"I will not be a pity fuck or a one-night stand. We do this, and you're mine. Are we clear?"

"I know. Please?"

"God help me, I can't say no to you," he growled, grasped the back of my neck and pulled me into a searing kiss.

Chapter Nine

Ronan

I'm in heaven and hell at the same time. The second my lips touched hers, I knew I was lost forever. Her arms wrapped around me so tightly, pressing her full body against mine. Her whimper against my lips enflamed me. Reflexively, I threaded a hand up into her hair while the other slid down her spine.

I tore my lips from hers on a groan, gulping lungfuls of air. Never have I ever been so wound up by just a kiss before. Her nails running through my hair sent tingles along my scalp.

Jesus Christ, she's going to make me come in my jeans if she doesn't stop.

Gripping her by her hips, I settled her on the edge of the countertop, slotting my hips between her thighs and relishing in the friction between us. Her squeak of surprise morphed into a moan before she wrapped her legs around me, pulling me tighter. Across my back, she flexed her fingers, inching my shirt higher. The dueling sensations of our fevered skin touching each other and the cool air hitting my back sent a shiver down my spine.

"God, Em," I bit out, dropping an open kiss against her neck, breathing in the sweet smell of her perfume and shampoo and just *her*.

"Too many layers," she grumbled while struggling to rip my shirt over my head.

"Slow down, baby. We have all night." Her whimpered response was all I got in response. "I'm not going anywhere, and I plan on taking my time with you."

"You mean that?"

"I do. I'll spend all night showing you if you need me to."

Her feral, excited grin was all I needed to grip her off the counter and carry her out of the room. My knee will hate me for it later, but for now, I don't care.

Fuck teammate bro code, rebuilt knees, or regrets.

Chapter Ten

Emory

I don't know what I expected out of Ronan, but this? This dominant, forward guy? Yeah, I wasn't expecting that. Laying me down gently, warm hands spread across my back, while settling me exactly where he wanted me, I couldn't help but compare the contrast between him and Kyle.

Kyle would have left the lights off and made quick work out of...whatever it was he wanted.

Ronan made sure the lights were on and hadn't taken his eyes off of me once.

Kyle would have touched me as little as possible.

Ronan couldn't keep his hands off of me.

I felt cherished, dare I say loved, by his every move. Was it too soon? Maybe. But after months of being touch starved, I deserve this, right?

"Are you still with me, Em?" Ronan's gravelly voice broke into my spiraling thoughts, his hands stilling on my ribs. "We can stop. I don't want to rush you."

"Don't you dare," I growled, locking my arms and legs around him before he can pull away.

"Then stay." A hot kiss dropped below my left ear, sending shivers down my spine.

"Here." Another one landed at my collarbone.

"With." Deft fingers slipped my bra below my breasts, so he could take one peaked nipple between his lips.

"Me." A shift to the other, so he could tease my heated flesh with a quick circle of his tongue.

"Oh God," I gaspped, the sensatings flooding my senses.

"Ronan will do just fine."

He holds my gaze steady, sliding a hand across the soft skin on my stomach. One place Kyle refused to look at or touch. I slam my eyes shut, afraid to see the disgust I had grown accustomed to.

"Eyes on me, baby girl." His tone left no room for arguement, and I couldn't help but obey. With a shaky breath, I cracked my ees open, watching his gleam as he watched me. "Don't hide, not from me. I want you to watch me worship you."

"But, I—"

"No buts about it. I'm not stopping until you forget his goddamn name and every shitty thing he said to you." Deft fingers tuck into my waistband, sliding the material down my thighs in one smooth movement. "I'm going to stay here until you forget your own name."

"You don't have to — I mean, it doesn't usually do any good."

He freezes, hands on my knees, carefully pressing them apart. "What?"

I sigh, embarassment flushing my cheeks. "I mean I can't — with that."

"You're saying you can't come if I eat you out?" I slammed my hands over my overheated face. He's so matter of fact about it. "No, none of that," he murmured, his hands gripping my wrists lightly, "I won't have you hiding from me. Tell you what," he paused, watching his own fingers sliding along my inner thigh. "Give me a few minutes. I've been dying to taste you for so long."

I fell back against the bedding, speechless. After being passed over and not considered, this feels foreign. I nodded my consent jerkily. His answering grin was feral as he lowered himself between my thighs, fingers spreading me wider as he digs in.

Sparks flew, my breath escaping me as he dropped an open-mouthed kiss against me, his tongue swiping through me. With a whimper, I grasped a handful of his hair, pulling him tighter. Hearing him groan in appreciation, I let the waves of sensation consume me, feeling something cresting bigger.

"Ronan, I—"

"Let it happen, gorgeous. You can do it."

Fireworks exploded behind my eyes as my orgasm took me over. Looking down at Rowan, grinning excitedly at me, I couldn't process the emotions and feelings.

"You..." I trailed off, panting breaths taking my words.

"No, sweetheart. You," he countered, crawling up my body like a wild animal.

Grabbing his head and kissing him felt as natural as breathing. He clearly agreed, giving in. Pulling away from me to step away from the bed, I felt the panic bubble in my chest a bit until I saw why. Opening up the drawer on his nightstand, he pulled out a condom, holding the foil in his teeth while reaching for his pants.

My shaking fingers reach out for his waistband, brushing against his happy trail.

"Next time, love," he whispers, bending down slightly to kiss my palm. Sliding his pants down in a quick motion, he carefully sheaths his length and climbs back into the bed. "I need to feel you."

Grabbing him around the neck, I swing so he's sitting, and I can straddle his thighs, pulling us close. Warm palms smooth down my hips, lifting me to settle onto his length.

"That's my girl," he groaned, leaning back. "You have no idea how hot you are right there, do you? So damn good." Praise and filth spilled from his lips, making my heart race. "Hold on tight," was all the warning he gave me before flipping us around, my back pressed into the soft bedding as he hovered over me, driving his hips into mine.

"Give me one more, sweetheart. I know you can," he growled, lifting me by my thighs to tuck a pillow under my back. The elevation changed his angle in a way that has my eyes rolling back in my head as he thrust deep, flicking his thumb against my clit. If I died, I'd die happy, that's for sure. "That's it, come for me."

As if on command, I did just that. My body pulled taught, and he followed me over the precipice.

My head is empty of thoughts, my muscles feel like jelly. With gentle hands, he pulls me close, kissing me softly as our breathing slows.

"We should get cleaned up, so we can go to bed" He climbs off the bed with a groan and a stumble, cursing "fucking knee" under his breath as he goes to dispose of the condom.

A quick shower later, and I found myself curled in Ronan's arms. I couldn't remember a time that I've ever been happier.

Chapter Eleven

Ronan

Waking up with Emory in my arms was ecstasy and agony at the same time. My knee screamed at me for the overexertion from the night before, but I couldn't even dwell on it. Her warm curves pressed against me? I wouldn't want to be anywhere else.

Carefully easing my arm out from underneath her, I made my way quietly down to the kitchen. The least I could do was take care of her, feed her, and then help her reassess in the cold light of day what actually transpired yesterday.

Settling into my morning routine calmed some of the anxiousness I had. I wanted to drive over to Kyle's house, beat the shit out of him, and gather every trace of Emory out of his house right this second, but I knew I needed to talk to her first. She might not want me to do it all or even have her stuff over here. I knew it wasn't my place to make these calls for her, even though I'd want nothing more than to set her up here and never let her go.

Soft hands wrapped around my stomach as I flipped an omelet. A satisfied feminine hum vibrates through my spine where she kissed me, holding me closer to her sleep-warm body.

"Good morning, gorgeous. How'd you sleep?"

"So good, until I woke up alone."

"Sorry, love. I tried to wrap this up so I could bring you breakfast."

"You were going to bring me breakfast in bed?"

"Yeah, where else would I bring you breakfast?" Her arms wrap around me tighter, and I swear I can feel a damp spot between my shoulder blades. "Em?"

"No one's ever — he never even—"

I set the spatula down carefully, withholding the urge to slam it down in frustration.

"He never made you breakfast?" Her head rolled side to side against my spine, to say no. "What kind of piece of shit — Em, come here, love."

Carefully, I try to turn in her tight grasp. Her watery eyes locked on mine, and my heart clenched.

I swear on all that's holy if I can keep her, I'm going to spoil the shit out of her.

"I was stupid to stay there."

"No, you thought he had redeeming qualities. There's a difference."

She sniffed, her eyes closing against the tears. Swiping away hot tears with my thumbs, I leaned down to press a soft kiss against her lips. "Pop up on the stool. Let me feed you. Mox is keeping him after practice for an extra workout, so we have time to get your things."

She pulled back in my hold, her eyes wide in horror. "Moxley knows? What did you tell him?"

"Just that you crashed here last night, and Kyle fucked up hard." I shrugged. "Just the important things. Oh, and Ronni wants you to call when you're settled in. She'd been after Kyle to get you in touch, and he apparently never remembered your number when she asked."

She snorted and rolled her eyes. "Of course not. I wonder what she needed to talk to me about?"

"Mox said she's been trying to expand her office and could use your skills if you wanted to work a regular job again."

"Are you serious? I would love to!"

The bright smile that exploded on her face made up for any hurt she felt. She was going to bounce back just fine after this.

Chapter Twelve

Emory

Walking into The Sin Bin felt different after staying with Ronan. I wasn't coming in to stress about follower count and analytics, scheduling conflicts or if some dude was going to yell at me for doing the thing that he wasn't capable of doing himself.

No, tonight I was walking in to see my boyfriend at his bar and watch the game with him. Walking into the warmth of the space, I heard the pre-game commentary already over the hum of conversation and laughter of the guests. Once again, Ronan's bar was the place to be. I smiled, thinking about how he had turned a bad experience into a good one, just like we did after mine.

I couldn't have imagined a better way to get over the heartbreak and stress that was Kyle.

However, those thoughts stuttered in my head as I saw Kyle slumped at the bar, Ronan leaning against the back counter, looking at him with his arms crossed and a frown on his face. Ronan had told me that Elliot warned him that something went down in the locker room and Kyle was on a

3-game suspension. However, I didn't think that would lead to my ex sitting in my boyfriend's bar tonight.

"Ronan?" His eyes shot to me andswiped hungrily from my hair to my boots and back before he walked toward the pass, motioning for me to meet him.

"He just walked in. I told him he can stay if he behaves and he doesn't say shit to you."

"Marking your territory?" I shot him a saucy look, so he would know I'm not mad about it.

"It's unnecessary. You're not property to own. Unless you want me to claim you." Even as he said it, he dropped a kiss against my knuckles with a wink. "But I won't make us a secret. You deserve to be loved out loud."

"Emory? What...Joey?" Kyle's voice broke our bubble of concentration, and I looked over Ronan's shoulder at him.

"What about it, Kyle?" I crossed my arms, daring him to say something.

"You left me for him? What the fuck!"

"He has a name, and to be fair, you left me first when you cheated. You didn't expect me to stick around and wait on you, right?" Ronan stood at my side, giving me the space to fight my battle, but close enough for support if I needed it. God, he's perfect.

"Fucking hell, Joey, what happened to bro code?" Kyle's words silenced nearby conversations, trying to pick up our arguement.

"Want to take this into my office? You're welcome to it. Just don't murder him in there."

"It's a tempting thought," I whispered back.

"That's my girl," he murmured, dropping a kiss against my temple before. "It's unlocked."

"Come on, Kyle. Quit making a scene." I keep walking

past him toward the stairs up to the office. feeling Ronan's eyes on me like a caress the entire time.

"Sit down. We need to talk." I motioned at the chair across from Ronan's desk and walked around to sit in Ronan's chair. The desktop between us felt like a physical and symbolic boundary between us. The cool leather that smelled so familiar gave me a boost of confidence. Ronan may not physically be here with me, but I could still feel him here.

"Emory, I need you to come back—"

"I'm sorry. Start over."

Kyle sat there, mouth gaping open as he froze mid-sentence. "Huh?"

"When people make mistakes or hurt someone, the right way to start an apology begins with 'I'm sorry.' Start over."

His eyebrows crunched in the middle of his forehead. "I don't understand."

"Of course you don't," I say with a sigh, eyes rolling at his insolence. He really wasn't the smartest out there. "Normal people would start this conversation by saying they were sorry for hurting the other person. But you really aren't."

"Emory, I've been under stress and now, with the suspension, I'm in real trouble."

"Again, not my problem. You made decisions, and these are the consequences."

"I need you to fix everything. How am I supposed to do this without you?"

"Still not my problem. You hurt and betrayed me." I paused, grinning. "I'm working for Veronica Snow now and I have to tell you, she pays way better than you ever did. He respects me. He honors my requests. He doesn't treat me like a servant. I'm actually happy again." My gaze drifts away from him, to the bar downstairs. "And honestly, Ronan has taken better care of me in the last couple of weeks than you had in the last year."

Kyle's eyes widen as realization hits. "You seriously left me for a has-been."

"Just because you're still on the roster for the moment and he's not, doesn't make you a better person."

"But you're my girlfriend!" His outburst should have sounded strong and powerful, but it just sounded petulant and whiny. God, why did I spend so much time attached to this?

"No, I'm not, Kyle. I used to be, but I'm not. You gave up on that claim when you turned me into unpaid help and brought another woman into our bed. Do I want to know how often you did that?"

His gritted teeth and pursed lips give me all the answers I need. She wasn't the first, just the first one I knew of.

"Do us both a favor. Lose my number. Don't talk to me, don't seek me out, don't even look in my general direction. I hope you get sent to the farm team, so I don't have to see you again. Move on. Leave us alone."

Kyle went pale, the curse of being sent to the minors scaring him more than anything.

"You don't really mean that."

"I do, Kyle. I'm done. I've been done. And frankly, I'm moving on to bigger and better." A giggle escapes me before I add, "Way bigger, and way better."

Angry red crept up from the collar of his shirt, and without another word, he stormed out of the room, slamming the door behind him.

I realeased a long, shaky breath. It was finally over. The conversation that we've needed to have now is over with, so

I could breathe freely. My lips curled into a small, satisfied smile. It's over. No tears shed, and I'm actually happy again.

The door creaked, and I looked over to see Ronan peeking through the crack.

"I saw him leave. Are you okay?"

"I couldn't be better," I answered truthfully, smiling in relief for a moment, before frowning. "Wait, I take that back."

His relieved smile fell at my amended statement. "What's wrong? How can I fix it?"

"Come here and kiss me."

"Gladly," he countered, coming up to the edge of the desk, eyeing me appreciatively. "I should have you sitting behind my desk more often, I think."

"Oh, yeah?"

"Yeah, especially in those boots. Have I told you they're my favorite yet?"

"No. Maybe you should, though."

Leaning over me with his hands braced against the armrests, he pressed a kiss along my jawline, teasing me with the soft touch. "Sit on my desk and I'll show you how much."

Yeah, I will not be tired of Ronan Josephs soon.

Home Ice Advantage

Introduction

So, this is a break from my usual programming. This technically started off as a very facetious chat with another author I love, Irene Bahrd. A light comment about how certain public figures are just "daddy" material, in a totally respectful way, turned into an entire "hear me out..." moment.

The next thing I knew, I was knee-deep in an age-gap short we dubbed "Senator Daddy." What if one of those aesthetically pleasing public figures on the correct side of the fight had a bit of a text conversation with a cam girl... who just so happened to be the coach's daughter? Still tied to hockey, but just a fun little short.

It worked out well, because I had already decided to put this book together, but I wanted something new in it. It's all well and good to give you the out-of-print snippets, but what about for everyone who already read them? So, Senator Daddy (or Home Ice Advantage) was formed.

It jumps time a bit, just as a heads up. Honestly, Ellie and Jack were trying their best to get a full book out of me. They still might, because there's still more from the chat that didn't make it in. They have history before Chapter One, and honestly, that Epilogue leaves everything wide open. Still, it was a fun dip into writing waters that I don't normally wade into!

I hope you enjoy spending some time with Ellie and Jack.

Love, Eden

Chapter One

Ellie

Sometimes, coming to a home game feels like going back in time. I swear to God, if I get offered another non-alcoholic beverage while being talked to like I'm a 12-year-old again, I'm going to fucking scream.

I should feel like I belong in the family box on home ice. I've watched games here since they hired my dad to coach the Ice Wolves a decade ago. The head office staff have known me for the majority of my life. Instead, I feel infantilized. I've been out of college for an entire year. I guess it's to be expected growing up in this arena, honestly. I'm in my twenties, I'm a fucking legal adult, but they still treat me like I'm that gangly kid trailing behind her daddy.

I haven't been that girl in a long, long time.

My phone buzzes in my hand, and I sigh in relief as I see my best friend's name flash across the screen, obscuring our graduation photo together. She's my ride or die, my "if we aren't married to anyone before we turn thirty, we're getting a Golden Girls bungalow together."

"Girl, where the hell are you? I thought you were

coming to the game with me!" Kimmy and I are light years beyond social niceties.

"Sorry, babe, my mom needed me for a photo op. Some children's charity event or something. I'll hang with you after?"

"Damn it. That sucks, I miss you," I grumble, looking at the Jumbotron to calculate how much longer until I'd see her again. "I swear, if I get offered another vodka soda without the vodka again with a wink, I'm going to lose it," I whisper into my phone, eyeballing the stakeholder who did just that earlier with some off-the-cuff comment about it being a school night, of all things. The tone echoed in my head, he liked the idea of school nights a bit too much. Maybe he's into the school girl thing, but that's not my jam.

After we end the call, I wander to the edge of the family space, looking down at the ice. The first period is well underway, and the Ice Wolves look solid this year, all high on the power play from a quick fight. It's just another Saturday night – I've been here hundreds of times.

I shift my gaze around at the stands to the proud fans sporting jerseys and Ice Wolves hoodies, cheering loudly. People-watching has always entertained me. It's also given me ideas for my upcoming marketing internships. Watching the fans interact with the various hype events during commercial breaks gives me ideas on what to suggest in the future. Sneaking a peek at the neighboring boxes, it's curious how different the lower bowl fan base reacts to the game, versus the luxury boxes. I pause, my observation falling on the box to my right.

At first glance, it looks like a group of older tech bros. Middle aged men in a uniform of polo shirts and khakis, high fiving each other with one hand while holding pale beers or rocks glasses in the other. While the self-congratulatory group chats amongst themselves, one man sits to the side by himself.

His dark hair has streaks of silver through it, and there's the faintest hint of shadow along his sharp jawline. He seems taller than the rest, and his white button down and dark slacks stand out against the sea of khakis and polos.

A silver fox, in the wild. Color me impressed.

Older men have always been more attractive to me than guys my own age. Maybe it's their maturity, or the ability to think past their own wants and needs. A rebellious thought hit me, and I can't help but let the daydream grow: What if the silver fox in the box beside me was like Daddy? A sliver of guilt passes through me. I don't know his name or what he looks like, just the screen name of Daddy.

I quickly swipe on the phone before I can talk myself out of it. Camera on, I take a series of photos and short videos, capturing my best angles. Some light edits later, and then I'm uploading to my secret subscription site.

And now I wait.

Chapter Two

Jack

I don't know why I let my office talk me into this. Sure, I like hockey, but this wasn't how I wanted to spend my Saturday night. Not that I had a ton of say in the matter. Rubbing elbows and getting my name out there is all that all matters. Networking has to come before anything else until the election, and it will probably get worse after that.

Mindlessly scrolling on my phone while my top donors are distracted, I try to ignore the avalanche of notifications popping up. Requests for interviews, another text rescheduling dinner with my daughter, and...

What's this?

IcePrincess has posted a new image.

Well, this is an interesting turn of events.

I glance around, making sure that no one is paying attention to me. With a quick swipe, I have the app open and there she is – my Princess.

At my age, maybe I should be ashamed of using an app like this. Paying for a subscription for photos of half-naked women – more specifically, this half-naked goddess – probably would destroy my career aspirations, but the risk is worth the reward.

Especially with the photo she just posted.

It isn't even overly sexy or revealing, but that tease of skin makes my heart pound. A pic shot from above, aimed into her ample cleavage, framed by a blue Ice Wolves varsity jacket.

Yeah, I'd recognize those tits anywhere.

As I've done for months now, I open up the app to leave her a large tip.

I'd give her a large tip, alright.

Jesus, quit thinking like a caveman.

It grants me access to a chat window to see her message pop up first.

> IcePrincess: Thank you, Daddy.

> Me: Is my pretty little princess enjoying showing off in public?

> IcePrincess: Just for you.

> Me: Show me how short that skirt is.

I look back out toward the game as the home team scores again, taking it to 4-0. It's just a preseason game, but the imbalance makes the night boring. My phone hums against my palm; at least someone is keeping me entertained.

A new private video posted for you.

I smirk as the words flash on my screen. I take a quick

glance to make sure the few people left in my box aren't paying attention, and open the app again. Her legs are crossed, only a hint of thigh showing, and then she moves. The angle changes slightly as her legs uncross, thighs parting and lifting the skirt higher, before recrossing again. Black knee high boots and bare thighs are my absolute weakness. It's a ridiculous thought, but fantasizing that she wears it just for me, drives me crazy.

What piques my interest even more than the absolute perfection she has on display, is the background—a luxury box identical to mine.

She's here.

I scan the boxes near me, seeking out a flash of her jacket among the sea of hockey sweaters. Adrenaline courses through my veins as I consider how close we are. What are the odds that I could see her in person or...touch her?

Oh, what I would give to touch her.

My eyes catch on a curvy brunette sitting in the box to my left. She's sitting by herself, scrunched low in the seats, the rest of the box full of people behind her.

Is that her?

I fire off a flirty message, keeping it light.

> **Me:** Showing off your pretty thighs in public. The things I would do to you…

> **IcePrincess:** Too bad you're not. What would you do, Daddy?

I choose my next words carefully. This can either go so right, or so wrong. I hold my breath and push send.

> **Me:** Who says I'm not?

IcePrincess: I don't believe you.

Oh, sweet girl, you have no idea what you've just done. My fingers fly across my screen in response.

Me: I should warm that fine ass of yours for that, Princess. However, since you insist….

I snap a picture of the scoreboard, attaching it to the text.

Her thumbs hover over the screen. Fuck, I said too much, she's going to call for security any moment now. She freezes, her wide eyes locked on her screen, teeth pressing into her bottom lip.

And then she types.

IcePrincess: You're really at the game too, Daddy?

Chapter Three

Ellie

He's here. Somewhere. Why else would he say that?

My heart flutters wildly against my ribs, the idea that my favorite patron is here– somewhere – and can see me, but I can't see him. I look around at the fans, wondering who it could be. Could it be the silver fox in the box beside me?

It would be perfect if that was him, but he's not paying attention to me.

> Daddy: What would you do if I was at the game?

It couldn't be him. I watch the silver fox drop his phone into the pocket of his dress pants, his attention turned back to the game. Disappointment settles in my belly. Well, it was a fun daydream.

> Me: I don't know, Daddy. What should I do?

Daddy: I want to see what you would do.
You're in the VIP suites, right? I recognize
the background in your photo.

Me: Yes.

Daddy: Go to the bar in the mezzanine.
Wait for me there.

This is either the smartest or stupidest thing I've ever done. Best case? The security here is top notch and he'd be escorted out of here immediately—probably banned for life.

Before I can talk myself out of it, I get up from my seat, walk into the box, and say my goodbyes to the staff and their family.

I try to casually walk toward the bar, sliding nervously onto a barstool. The bartender hands me my usual cranberry vodka – thank god, someone around here knows I'm of age – and I try desperately to present a casual facade that I do not feel at all.

Not cool, calm, collected. More like hot, bothered, and excited.

The idea of meeting a patron should scare the shit out of me, but I feel totally safe here at the arena, and there's a thrill in the unknown that I cannot deny. Who is he? Is he attractive? We've talked on the app a lot, but that doesn't mean I know him that well, though. Meeting up with a stranger feels illicit, it's forbidden. Maybe I should walk away, no one will know—

"Ice Princess?" His voice feels like warm chocolate against my senses, and I pause my stirring.

He's here. He's standing behind me. He's here and he can see me and–

Turn around, Ellie. Quit acting like an idiot and turn around.

I spin slowly, my eyes trained on the ground as his shoes enter my periphery. Expensive shoes at that, Well-tailored black pants, and a crisp white shirt tucked in at a trim waist, sleeves cuffed just below his elbows.

How did you get abducted, Ellie? Forearm porn.

Focus, shit.

I lift my gaze, taking in his unbuttoned collar, strong jawline, and dark hair streaked with silver.

Jesus Christ, Daddy is the silver fox I lusted over during the first period.

"Hi."

"Hi? Just 'hi,' Princess?"

I shake my dick-addled brain– because what else could it be, really– and try it again. "Hi, Daddy."

"May I?" he asks politely, motioning to the empty stool beside me.

"Oh! Yes, please."

Can you be any more awkward? Holy hell.

He waves down the bartender, ordering a top shelf whiskey and a new drink for me, before turning toward me.

"So, do you come here often?" We make eye contact, and then he drops his head, cheeks turning ruddy. "Please forget that I asked that, damn, that was cheesy."

A giggle escapes my lips and I try to hide my smile behind my glass. "I do come here often, actually. You might say that this is the family business."

"Oh really? That's an unusual legacy. Which part?"

"Um, well..." She sips her drink, then looks sideways at me. "My dad's the coach."

"You're– you're what? How did I not notice that?

"That's why a lot of my videos are faceless. He can't know about the... well, you know.."

"I should have known. It isn't your first time in that jacket, if I remember right."

"It's my favorite." I grin, my shoulders shimmying.

"It might be mine, too," I catch him mumbling against the rim of his glass.

"Excuse me?"

"You know what I said," he retorts with a laugh. "I can't seem to keep my cool around you. Any other time, I know just the right thing to say."

"I don't see a problem with it," I return, turning so my bare knee rubs against his own.

"What are the odds of us running into each other like this," he muses, his palm warm against my thigh.

"I'm sure it would have happened at some point. This really isn't that large of a city."

His phone chimes on the bar top, and with an apology, he glances at the screen.

"That's surprising," he muses. "Apparently everyone in my box decided to head out. A five goal lead was sufficient for them."

"They just left you behind? Some friend group they turned out to be."

"They weren't really my friends, it was just a networking opportunity. My assistant was letting me know he had my things."

"Oh, do you need to go catch up with them? I don't mean to keep you back."

"You're far better company than they ever were, Princess. Don't sell yourself short like that."

I can't stop the smile on my face. "That's sweet of you to

say, but I mean, truly, it was lovely to meet up. Maybe it can happen again later."

"Or, it doesn't have to end at all." His eyes lock on mine. "No one is in the box, we can go back there."

"That actually sounds really nice."

He settles the tab at the bar, then stands, holding his hand out for me. I feel sparks as I make contact with his palm, his grip closing lightly on mine before lifting our joined hands to his lips placing an electrifying kiss between my knuckles.

I gasp, the roughened rasp of his stubble and the softness of his lips throwing my senses into disorder. Stepping down off of the barstool with a wobble, I gather my phone.

"You good, Princess?"

"Fine." It's breathless, so I clear my throat a bit, and repeat, "Yeah, I'm fine."

His eyes skate down my body, his gaze almost touching me as it travels from my face, down my heaving chest, to where my thighs are pressed together."

"Damn right, you are." He pulls my hand up to his mouth again, this time to scrape his lips along the pulse on my wrist, drawing a whimper from me.

A whimper? What kind of sorcery is this? I don't do that!

Without another word, he pulls me toward his box. All I can think is this may be the best damned idea I've had in a long time.

Chapter Four

Jack

I close the door behind us, just as the goal horn blares again, the strobing lights placing Ellie in a silhouette in front of me. Never in my wildest dreams would I have thought of her here with me, alone.

"Come here." My command is soft, but her reaction is immediate. She steps closer, her head tilting up to meet my eyes. "We're going to watch the last period and then we're going to dinner. Okay?"

"Yes, Daddy." Her forehead crinkled in confusion.

"You have questions?"

"I – I thought..."

"What? You thought I would take you in here and fuck you against the wall, like a common whore?"

"Y-yes, Daddy."

"Is that really what you want from me, Princess?"

"N-no."

"Say it again."

"No, Daddy."

"Tell me what you really want."

"I –"

Her lips press together, holding in words. I can see her trying to present that same confident persona that she uses on her page. My Princess, such a shy little thing offline.

"If you want me to touch you, Ellie, you're going to have to say it."

"Touch me, Daddy. Please."

"Stand at the rail behind the seats. Hold on tight. Feet apart. And don't make a sound or I'll stop." She nods her head quickly. "That's my good girl."

My pulse pounds in my ears, watching her follow my instructions. Her steps seem timid as she approaches the railing, and I feel panic start to rise in me. Maybe I was wrong, maybe she isn't into this. She's going to run out of the box to security, and... But I freeze, watching her reservations melt around her, confidence taking over her posture. Her spine straightens, and the slight little wiggle of her hips makes her skirt swish around her thighs.

So damned perfect.

I step up behind her, pulling her hair over her left shoulder and exposing her neck. She sighs, shifting lightly back, as her curves molding to me. The press of her ass against my already hard cock is delicious, but I need to rein it in.

"You're a touch-starved little thing, aren't you?" I whisper in her ear, dropping a kiss behind her lobe. She shivers in response, her restless shifting morphing into a full grind against me.

"Maybe."

"You want me to touch you here, where anyone could look in and see us? Your father is right there, just yards away. What would he say if he saw you?"

"I don't care. Please, please touch me."

"Dirty girl, rubbing yourself on me like that. What

would you do if I left you like this all night? I'm not fucking you. Not yet, and not here." Her gasp is music to my ears, and I wish for a moment that we weren't in a public venue. I slide my hand along the back of her thigh, relishing in the feel of her muscles twitching under my fingertips, reflexively trying to close on my hand. "Stay right there. Princess. Do as you're told or I won't touch you."

Chapter Five

Ellie

My heart is going to beat out of my chest and I'm going to die before he ever lays a proper finger on me.

And who knew that prim and proper Jack Winslow in public was also bankrolling my platform, but was also this dirty talking demon.

"Such a good girl."

Seeing his praise in a text? That's cool.

Hearing him growl it in my ear while I grind against his hard dick? There are no words. A whimper escapes me, my knees buckling slightly.

Never have I ever folded like a cheap lawn chair, until now.

And here we are.

"What are you doing to me, Princess?" he growls in my ear, the vibration of his words resonating through my back. "You and this little cocktease of a skirt."

"Sorr–oh!" I gasp as he dips a finger under the seam of my panties. His deep hum of approval as he drags that digit through the slickness has me biting hard on my lip, trying to keep my sounds inside.

"You're making a mess of yourself over here." He slides in, out, and circles my clit, making my eyes roll back in my head. "Sitting over there, thinking of this, getting all worked up for me, hmm?"

A gasp escapes me as he circles my bundle of nerves again. "Yes, Daddy," I whisper, willing my knees to stay steady.

"And what were you planning to do, after sending me that tease of a video? Were you going to run home and do this to yourself?"

"Most likely," I try to chirp before he changes his rhythm. "Oh god, yes, I would."

"Would you have sent it to me?" Another slide, another dip.

Where did this man learn to do that? My knees wobble as sensation overwhelms me. He's going to do it, he's going to make me come harder than I have in my entire adult life and I just met him, and he hasn't touched me with anything but his fingers. "If you asked."

"You wouldn't have enjoyed it nearly as much, though," he muses. "You're leaking all over my hand and you're not even done yet."

"So close," I whisper, trying to regulate my breathing before I pass out.

"I know you are. And the game is almost over. You have five seconds before the horn blows and no one can hear you getting off on my fingers. Are you ready?"

Am I ready? Dude has no idea.

I glance up through my lashes, watching the scoreboard.

It hits zero. The horn blows. The crowd cheers, and in a VIP box, my knees buckle and I scream.

"Thank you, Daddy," I gasp, as I try to gather my scattered thoughts.

"You're welcome, Princess." He rests his back against the chair, sucking my release off his finger. "Now, let's get you put together. I promised you dinner."

Chapter Six

Jack

Taking Ellie to dinner on a Saturday night like she's any other date shouldn't feel like that big of a deal, so why am I nervous? It's not like it's our first time seeing each other, she dryhumped my leg at the arena last week. I shake the thought away, take a fortifying breath, and restlessly smooth out invisible wrinkles in my pants. I should've picked her up, but she said she would meet me here; it feels like a chump move, but is this what dating is like now?

She comes across the restaurant toward me, head held high, and all eyes on her. Her lips quirk up at the corners in a soft smile as she approaches. The little black dress she's wearing makes my mouth dry. I stand from our table, cutting the distance between us. I can't stay away from her for another second.

"Princess, you're ravishing tonight," I praise as I pull her close.

"Thank you Daddy," she murmurs, leaning into my touch.

I don't think I will ever get enough of how touch

addicted she is. Pulling out a chair for her, I admire her dress as she sits, the hem of the skirt giving me just a tease of thigh as she crosses her legs.

"I took the liberty of ordering us some wine, unless you'd prefer something else?" I start to wave down the waiter when she gently pulls my hand down by my wrist.

"No, wine is perfect. Thank you."

I sigh in relief, filing her glass before taking my own seat beside her. "I'm so glad you were able to come out with me tonight, I figured you would be busy."

"With what?" Her head tilts in confusion. "I typically don't like going out a lot. It's so crowded and overstimulating sometimes."

"Don't you usually post a video on Saturday nights?" The words fall smoothly from my lips, and I freeze. We've never outright talked about her site.

"I pre-record and schedule the post days in advance. That way, if anything comes up, I'm not late." The answer falls effortlessly from her lips. "Stockpiling batches also gives me something to fall back on if I'm not feeling well, or just not feeling like it this time."

"That's smart," I compliment, sipping my wine.

"Well, I do have a rabid fan base."

My eyes shoot up to hers, just to watch the impish glean in her eye. She's poking fun at me, clearly. "Some of us just have very specific standards," I shoot back, winking.

"Slightly demanding, sometimes?"

"Cheeky," I warn, raising an eyebrow.

"Sorry, Daddy. It's all in good fun."

"Have you ever considered going mainstream? I mean, your photos are beautiful, there has to be a market for it."

"I'm 5'3" and curvy, I don't fit the aesthetic elsewhere,"

she answers, her tone going bitter. "It could be worse, I suppose. I could not have a creative outlet at all."

"We are not going to subscribe to that ideal," I growl. "You're perfect, and sexy. The opinions of a few fatphobes should never play a part in your opinion. Say it again."

"Sorry, what?"

"Tell me what you are." I need to calm down, my tone feels too biting for this. But damnit, society has her convinced that she isn't worthy of anything outside of this platform? I'm pissed. I'm pissed for her, not at her, but I have nowhere to direct this.

"I-I'm...sexy?"

"And perfect."

She chuckles. "I'm not going to say that. It feels like a step too close to conceited."

"You're sexy and..." I roll my fingers in a circle so she'll continue.

"Perfect," she whispers.

"Again. Louder."

"I'm sexy and...and perfect."

"Good girl," I praise. "Now don't forget that. Or do I need to spank it into you?"

Her cheeks flush as she tries to hide a smile behind her wine glass.

"Thank you, Daddy."

"Now tell me, what else my beautiful girl has been up to lately?"

Chapter Seven

Ellie

Waking up in Jack's arms, pulled tight against his larger frame, feels like heaven..

Stretching with a soft moan, I press closer to his sleeping form, smiling at his soft snore. His sleep-warm skin shifting away as his hands shift, make me shiver as the heat is replaced by the cool air in the room.

"Good morning," he drawls in my ear as I brush against him one more time. "I could get used to this."

"Me too," I sigh, gasping as his thick fingers coast across my nipple, pulling slightly, sending shockwaves through me. He's way too good at this.

When he trails his hand down to my aching clit, my brain short circuits. I'm gone. No one finds my favorite spots as quickly as me – except for him.

"Spread those thighs open for me, Princess."

I obediently hinge my hip, sliding my calf along his while giving more space for his hand. He hums contentedly in my ear, dipping a fingertip into my wetness before drawing it back up to my clit again. He shifts behind me, his length sliding alongside his fingers, a tease of what I could have.

"Let me in, sweet girl," he murmurs. His blunt head slips away once, twice, before he thrusts home. We moan in sync as he rocks, his finger moving against my clit in counterpoint to his hips.

I'm going to come faster than I ever have in my entire life and it's this man in control of it. I don't know how I can ever move on to mediocre dick after this. My muscles begin to spasm around him, my cries growing incoherent the higher he pushes me.

"That's it, come on Daddy's dick, good girl," he praises, running kisses along my neck.

I'm lost. I shatter, feeling myself flutter around him, the sounds of our flesh slapping together getting louder as he thrusts deeper, harder, and faster, keeping me balanced in this freefall state of orgasm. He grunts, shifting me onto my belly and pressing in deeper. "That's it, give me one more."

"Yes, so good," I moan, my eyes drifting shut as I ride out the feeling.

His arms band around me, pulling me tight against him as he groans my name, pressing hot kisses along my shoulder. Our breaths sync as they slow, and I just start to drift back to sleep when the thud of a distant door slamming disrupts the silence.

"Daddy, I'm home!"

We freeze.

"Who is—"

"Fuck!" he hisses in my ear.

Chapter Eight

Jack

My body screams as I jump from the bed, and I curse as my back twinges. While Chloe is a grown adult, I don't want to have to explain or make introductions with Ellie while she's mostly naked and covered in the evidence of our lovemaking.

"Daddy?" Chloe's voice calls up the stairs, closer than before.

"Shit, she's coming upstairs."

Ellie squeaks, flings the covers back, and runs into my bathroom. Without even turning on the light, she pulls the door closed behind her, leaving only a crack to look through.

"Just a minute," I yell toward the door.

I finish tugging a pair of sweats on and glance back toward the bathroom door, just to watch her arm squeeze through the widening crack, waving at me to go. I wipe my sweaty palm on my thigh before grabbing at the doorknob, my shaky hand sliding off the cool metal before I can properly open it. My daughter is on the opposite side, with her hand wrapped around the knob. I stare at her hand, the realization weighing heavy on my gut—she's going to walk into my bedroom regardless of what I said.

"Chloe, what are you doing here?"

"I tried to call you, and you didn't answer. We should do brunch."

"Right now. You let yourself into my house to tell me we should go out with absolutely no warning?"

"Well, you would have had warning if you answered your phone," she retorts, rolling her eyes. Her arms cross her chest, her fingers tapping on her arms impatiently while she waits.

"I was sleeping, it's the weekend and for the first time in weeks I don't have anything scheduled. You could have told me this last night when you texted–"

"What's that?" She interrupts, her gaze on the floor by my bed.

At a pair of lacy panties.

"Look, will you just go downstairs, I'll meet you in a minute."

"Is there someone here with you?" I press my lips shut, not satisfying her with an answer. "Daddy!" Her screech echoes off the walls as she pushes past me, looking around.

"What the hell are you doing? Stop!" I grab for her arm as she dodges past me, tossing open my closet door before heading for the bathroom door. "I said stop!"

She ignores me, smacking the unlatched door with her hand hard enough for it to bounce off the wall and revealing Ellie huddled in the shower, wrapped in my robe.

"Who the hell is this?" my daughter screams, gawking at Ellie.

"I told you to go downstairs. I mean it. Go." The demand hisses through my gritted teeth,

"She's my age! What kind of sick shit is this?"

"Chloe, I told you to go downstairs and I mean it," I roar. "Get out, now."

Her eyes narrow, and with one last disdainful look between the two of us, she storms out, screaming about how she can never come home again.

Sighing tiredly, I pull Ellie toward me, allowing her soft curves to comfort me, and hope I provide some comfort to her as well. She pulls back slowly, never taking her eyes off of the floor.

"You should go after her. I'll go home."

"No, you're not. You're staying. She's in the wrong here."

"But she's your daughter, you need to work this out. It's fine, Jack."

She never calls me that and my heart aches. Her face is pale as she gathers her clothes from the floor, throwing them on quickly.

"Wait, Princess, we–"

"It was fun. Okay?" she snaps. "Let's just leave it at that."

My shoulders droop in defeat, watching her storm out of the room. Maybe the time is wrong, maybe she's right.

But damnit, I'm going to get my girl back, even if it kills me.

Chapter Nine

Ellie

The problem with meeting the best guy in the world? There's always something to keep you apart. Everything that I loved prior to our amazing weekend now feels bland, colorless.

Sitting at brunch with Kimmy a week later, I still miss him. We barely dated, why is this hitting me so hard?

It wasn't just a weekend. He's always been there in the app. Or had been. His account closed after I left. I cried in a bubble bath, reading through the messages from "Unknown User" until the water ran cold.

I sigh, shoving a sliced strawberry around on my plate. There's not enough champagne in my mimosa to deal with my messy feelings.

"Are you still bummed about last weekend?" Kimmy asked, spearing a chunk of cantaloupe. "He's just a guy. You can replace him. Or hit him with your car."

"I don't want to hit him with my car," I grumble, sipping the oversweet mixture in my glass. "I wanted to keep him, if anything. He was sweet, kind, and caring. A freaking gentleman! Do you know how hard it is to find a grown man who puts your needs first?"

"I do. Why do you think I'm swearing off boys and only dating girls right now."

I salute her with my glass. "That's a solid plan. The dating scene is fucking bleak."

"Ellie?"

I turn too quickly for the amount of alcohol in my system, sending the restaurant on a tilt-o-whirl around me.

"Hi. Um, can I help you?" I recognize her as Jack's daughter, but we've never officially talked. Ever.

"I'm sorry to interrupt, it's just," she trails off, and chews on her bottom lip. "Could we talk?"

I motion at the empty seat at our table, and start a wordless conversation with my friend.

It's her. *That's the daughter*, I say telepathically to Kimmy, darting my eyes at her as she settles into the seat. My friend's eyes go wide, her gaze fixed on the newest addition to the table. I don't miss the appraising look in her eyes.

Don't even think about it. My eyes narrow in warning. I smile at his daughter, attempting to be cordial. "I don't think we were ever properly introduced," I start, holding my hand out to her. "I'm Ellie."

"Chloe. I'm so sorry about our last meeting. I kind of overreacted when I saw you there."

"I'm sure it was a bit of a shock. I probably would have done the same if I wasn't expecting someone in my dad's house."

"He's dated before," she sighs, her cheeks turning red. "It's been a long time, but he's never dated someone so close to my age before. It was... surprising."

"We're both consenting adults," I counter.

"But what would you have done if your dad had someone your age in his bed?"

"Would I have been upset? Initially, maybe. But it's not my place to pick who he dates."

She hangs her head. "I guess it was a shock, I wasn't expecting this."

"Understood. If it's any consolation, I don't think it will happen again. Or at least not with me."

"This is going to be awkward, but about that... Would you talk to him again? As much as it bothers me that he'd been with someone old enough to be his daughter too, he was happy. You made him happy. He's been a mess since that morning."

"What do you want from me?"

She takes a breath, her eyes closed.

"Call him. See him. Something. I shouldn't have said anything to you that morning and that's on me. He shouldn't have to suffer because I couldn't be a grown-up about it."

"I'll think about it."

Her shoulders relax a bit and the three of us stare at each other. "I should let you get back to this, but thanks for listening." She rises, walking off to a table of other girls watching from the opposite side of the restaurant.

"Well, that was certainly something," Kimmy muses, watching her walk away.

Chapter Ten

Jack

My pulse throbs in my temples as I sit through yet another meeting with my campaign manager. I get it, I do. I said I wanted to commit to this, I just wish Ellie was by my side for it.

My heart lurches in my chest as I remember our brief time together. I never should have let her walk out of my apartment, no matter what. Now, I'm lonely and miserable again and I have no one to blame but myself.

"Are you even listening to me?"

"What? Oh, um, sorry," I wince. " Go ahead, it sounds great."

"You don't even know what I just said."

He's not wrong. I have no idea what's going on around me.

"I'm so sorry, Mr. Winslow, but there is someone here who needs to speak with you." I glance up at my secretary, standing inside the doorway.

"Let's reconvene after lunch, maybe Jack will show up mentally after some food."

I groan, hanging my head over my laptop, fingers gripping my hair in frustration. Today has been a shit show of epic proportions and I can't bear the idea of disappointing yet another person–

"Hi."

My eyes shoot to the door, barely recognizing that my team had vacated the room and see her.

Ellie is standing inside my office doorway, black wrap dress hugging her curves, her hair pulled back in a low bun, and her ballet flats shifting nervously on the floor. Her shoulders hung low, her arms wrapped around herself. My girl is uncomfortable and I'm just standing here, staring at her like I've never seen her before.

"Ellie." Her name is barely a whisper, but her eyes still lock on me.

"Hi. Um, can we talk?" Her nose wrinkles adorably as she scowls. "I mean, can we maybe talk over lunch?"

"I'd love to," I answer her. Is she really here? Or am I just imagining her? We can order in, if you'd like. We can stay in my office. It would be quieter there."

My hand lands like a magnet on the small of her back. I can't stop myself from touching her, making sure she's actually here. Telling my assistant to order something from the cafeteria downstairs and bring it up to us, I finish guiding Ellie toward my office door. The silence that descends on the room as the door latch closes with a soft click is deafening.

"So, you wanted to talk," I start, reminding us both why we're here. And miserable.

"I should apologize," she starts. "I didn't give you a chance to explain before I left. I panicked, and thought it was better to just go."

"Oh, Princess, I understand. I didn't tell you that my

daughter drops by unannounced, and then she barged in on us.

"About that...did she tell you she found me at brunch the other morning?"

I shake my head. "She hasn't said anything recently, sorry."

"She talked to me. Actually, she apologized to me for barging in like that. I guess she felt bad because you had been so happy before that and since then,..."

"I missed you, Princess."

"I missed you too, Daddy."

A groan escapes me as I watch her, leaning back against my desk, pulling that scarlet painted bottom lip of hers between her teeth again. "You're killing me, you know that? The last few weeks have been torture."

"You shut down your account." Her statement is direct, but I can't miss the disappointment in her tone.

"I did," I admit. "I couldn't stay away."

"But you didn't say anything to me," she pouts.

"I know, I'm sorry." I step closer to her. "Is it too late for us to start over?"

"No, I think it's the perfect time for us."

I step back a bit, and hold out my hand. "Hi, I'm Jack."

She grins, her cheeks turning pink as she takes my hand in a polite handshake. "Hi, I'm Eleanor. But you can call me Ellie."

Emboldened by her touch, I tighten my grasp and pull her toward me, her shift in balance causing her to catch herself against my chest with her free hand. Without another word, I grasp her face with both hands, pulling her in for a kiss.

Epilogue

Ellie

I've always loved Thanksgiving. Gathering with family and friends, sharing comfort foods, and this is no exception. This year is really special, because Jack and his daughter are coming. This will be the first time our families have met.

Jack lounges on the couch, reading glasses perched on the end of his nose as he reads on his tablet. Those slutty little glasses make him exponentially hotter.

"Look at you, sitting there like a hot professor fantasy."

He looks up at me, smiling warmly before patting the couch beside him. I sit on the cushion beside him, enjoying the way he naturally shifts to rest his arm across my shoulders, like it's magnetized to me.

"Are you saying you want to roleplay when we go home?" he retorts, pulling me closer to him on the couch. "Alone at last."

"Shh, your daughter is around here somewhere," I admonish, trying to place a little distance between us. Just because everyone knows we're in a committed relationship, doesn't mean we need them to witness everything. And honestly, my dad approves of it, because I'm happy and Jack is an established, mature person; nothing like the boys I used to date. Jack's daughter still doesn't fully approve, but she says she tolerates it because he's happier than he had been in years.

"Where did Chloe go? I thought she came in here with you."

"She went to get more wine," he replies, fingertips twisting in the loose curls at the base of my neck.

"Maybe I should go find her, I feel like a poor excuse for a hostess leaving her to get her own."

I pop up, heading towards the kitchen to find her. Maybe Dad showed her the wine cellar, I wonder as I head toward the basement stairs. Voices drift from below as I step further into the cellar.

Familiar voices.

"What would your daddy say if he saw you like this..."

I freeze. Panic clenching my heart.

Oh my god. She didn't.

Acknowledgments

I have so many people to thank, and I'm always afraid I'll forget someone. My support network has grown immensely over the last couple years, and I couldn't be where I am now without any of you.

To my friends and family. I love you all. Thank you so much for letting me be authentically me, without judgement. Or at the very least, keeping your "wow, that girl is unusual" where I can't hear it! I know I started off my writing with "I'm writing a book, you don't have to read or acknowledge it" because let's be honest, I'm writing things you don't usually talk to your mama about. Or your scout leaders. And you're all usually one of the first ones to lay hands on the latest thing to pop out of my head. You have no idea how much this means.

To that tattooed man I married. He's the one who would hint that I had a book to write if I tried to avoid it. My behind-the-scenes support system. We may never see him at a book signing with me, but he's the one wrangling me back behind the keyboard. I love you so much!

To my Cincy Author Coven. From the group chats to brunches, this little circle of friends has been a solid source of support that will stare me in the face and talk me off the ledge, if needed. I always look forward to our gatherings, running amok through Joseph-Beth to find our books after brunch, attending book signings together, there's never a bad time! Love you ladies so much!

The Romance Riot! The Discord that started it all. Technical details, moral support, body doubling, you've all been there for it all. Kate, Liz, April, Sage, Rose, Elsie, thank you for always being a DM away to hear out all the dumb things that come out of my head, or walking me through problems. I'm so incredibly honored to be included in your orbit.

Irene gets her own line. This freaking woman, I tell you. Not only is she one of the best table neighbors, but she's an all around great person and author. Thank you for everything. For helping me flesh out "Senator Daddy," for being my niece's favorite author and being cool as she fangirled. You're one in a million, I hope you know that.

My heathens, readers who have taken a chance on an unknown author simply for "hockey" or "vibes," thank you so, so much for giving my little books some of your attention. As a voracious reader myself, even I get overwhelmed with the number of books on my TBR that I still haven't gotten to, and I know you have to feel the same. Thank you for giving space to my Ice Wolves. I don't have words to convey how much it means to a small indie author to be included in your precious reading time.

All my love,
Eden

About the Author

Eden Knox is a sports romance author who lives in Ohio with her 2 girls, herd of animals, and her "looks like could kill you, is a cinnamon roll" husband. When she isn't screaming at hockey or football games, she's working on tormenting her fictional hockey team or completing coursework for grad school. Currently, she is working on book 3 in The Sin Bin Series, Hooking Up With Number 36.

instagram.com/edenknoxwrites

facebook.com/eden.knox.145432

tiktok.com/@edenknoxwrites

Also by Eden Knox